LOVE TIES

Love Ties

An Unbreakable Bond

MARILYN FREEMAN

Spellbrooktales

ISBN: 9781739688080

First Printing, 2022

Publisher: Spellbrooktales

Website: www.spellbrooktales.com

Cover design by Marilyn Freeman

Contents

Prologue

May 2007

It was a glorious spring day. Jack had taken a few days of his annual holiday to do a bit of decorating. They'd lived here for seven years, and the place was beginning to look a bit shabby. Grace had decreed that something must be done. As his wife had a hair-dressing appointment that afternoon and weather was so perfect, Jack decided he would have a break from decorating to take Toby for a couple of hours at the beach.

'I'd rather you didn't,' Grace told him, 'on a day like this, the beach will be packed with day-trippers.'

'So what?' Jack said. 'Honestly Grace, you fuss too much over the lad. What harm can possibly come to him? It'll be good for him to see other children playing and splashing in the sea.'

'Well, I don't want him going in the sea, and that's final. I mean it Jack! It'll be full of all sorts of people and you never know...'

'Ok if it makes you happy. We'll just play in the sand.'

'Well don't forget to put plenty of suncream on him.'

Jack smiled to himself, poor Grace, she does fuss so. He knew why, of course. Toby was so precious to her, well, to them both, of course. They'd endured five years of trying to conceive, including several rounds of IVF with Grace twice becoming pregnant only to tragically miscarry after a few weeks. The health service in the area financed only three courses and they had paid for another two themselves, all to no avail, and they had to stop the IVF. As sometimes happens, once they relaxed and stopped fretting, to their joy and amazement Grace finally became pregnant naturally. They were obviously delighted, but still terrified she may miscarry again. Their anxieties continued throughout the pregnancy, but finally, in the spring of 2007, she gave birth to a healthy little boy, who they named Toby.

After Grace left for the hairdresser's, Jack packed the rucksack, strapped Toby in his pushchair and set off in the direction of the promenade. Grace had been right and the place was heaving. At the first sign of a bit of sunshine it seemed that half the world made a bee-line for the Tidmouth beach. Jack understood why, of course. There were three miles of golden sand fringing an expanse of safe, shallow water to be safely enjoyed by children of all ages.

They found a vacant spot on the beach not too far

from the Jubilee Memorial and settled down to enjoy their afternoon. Jack took out the bag of sand-toys he'd brought with them and began to build his son a sandcastle. Together, they decorated it with starfish and shell shapes, finally triumphantly planting a flag on the top. Then Toby was particularly happy filling up his tipper truck with sand then tipping it out again, apparently in a vain attempt to move the whole beach!

Jack was content as he watched his son. He had to admit he was a bonny lad, with fair curls and bright blue eyes, like his mother. The thought of Grace somewhat spoiled his mood. He did love her, of course, but the last few years had been very trying. The more obsessed she'd become with having a child, the more he had begun to feel that in her eyes his sole purpose was to give her what she craved. Their once wonderful and fulfilling intimate life had become something very different, just a means to an end, rather than an expression of their love for one another. During the years of IVF, gone was the glorious, spontaneous sex they had once enjoyed, then everything was governed by her hormone levels. Finally came the crushing realisation that they would probably never have a child of their own and Grace grieved the loss of hope. When she finally and unexpectedly became pregnant with Toby though, she completely lost interest in Jack, reinforcing his feeling that he had now fulfilled his only function and wasn't really needed any more.

The one consolation in all this of course, was Toby.

He was delightful, particularly now that he was beginning to chatter in that endlessly entertaining way two-year olds do. Now Jack watched his little boy grab a handful of sand, obviously delighting in the feel of it and the way it trickled through his podgy fingers. This afternoon at the beach had been a rare chance for him to be with his son. Grace never seemed to trust him to look after Toby alone. He was gazing lovingly at his little boy, whose face broke into an expression of sheer joy as he threw his hands up to scatter the sand in the air.

'Whoa! Don't throw it around son,' Jack gently admonished him, picking up the spade and showing him once again how to shovel sand into his bucket, finally tipping it out to make a sand-pie. Toby was delighted with the result, or rather with the opportunity it gave him to squash it flat, with a giggle.

'Right then!' Jack exclaimed as he grabbed him round his waist and started to tickle him. Toby was delighted and screamed excitedly.

'Come on young man, time to go!' Jack suddenly exclaimed, 'Mummy should be back from the hairdresser's now, and she'll expect us home for tea.'

He knelt down and started to pack the bucket and spade away, but Toby had other ideas and grabbed the spade, toddling off with it. Jack jumped up and went after him and was grateful that a young woman who had been sitting nearby had intercepted him, allowing time for him to be scooped up safely in his father's arms. Toby squealed his resistance and wriggled to escape his father's embrace.

'Oh no you don't, scamp!' he said, grinning, then thanked the woman and with some difficulty, managed to strap Toby into his pushchair. Gathering up the rest of their things, he stuffed them into the rucksack and set off across the sand and up the slope to the promenade.

Crossing the road, Jack remembered that Grace had asked him to pick up a bottle of milk on the way home and made for the convenience store at the corner of the block. The door was open, and Jack could see the milk in the fridge just opposite the counter. Parking the pushchair to the side of the door he stepped inside to take a bottle. Turning to the counter, he commented to the shopkeeper what a lovely day it had been, and, quickly paying for the milk, stepped outside.

As he emerged from the shop he was horrified! The pushchair was gone! Toby was gone! He ran backwards and forwards up and down the street calling his son's name. He ran into the shop, shouting to the shopkeeper,

'Did you see anyone!? Was there anybody outside while I was in here?!'

The man quickly replied that he hadn't seen anyone and asked him what the matter was.

'My son's gone!!' Jack exclaimed. 'He was right outside here but now he's gone! Someone must have taken him! Please, help me!'

He ran back outside and round the corner, crossing the street to get a better view down the side road, but to no avail. There was no sign of Toby's pushchair. His mind stopped working. He couldn't think what to do next. The man from the corner shop came out and asked what colour the pushchair was. Jack described it and the man said,

'You go that way towards the pier and I'll go down towards the marina. They can't have got far. You were only in the shop a few seconds.'

'OK,' said Jack, glad that someone had taken charge because he was in a complete panic, utterly unable to think what to do next. He ran along the prom as far as the pier, searching the crowded pavements, before the stitch in his side stopped him in his tracks. There was no sign of the pushchair. He stood with his hands on his knees, trying to get his breath back, when a Police Community Support officer came up to him and asked if he needed help.

'It's my son!' he exclaimed. 'Someone's taken him!'

'How do you mean, taken him?' she asked.

'I mean, stolen him!' Jack shouted, 'What do you think I mean!?'

'Ok. Where was he taken from?'

Jack gabbled that he had only stepped inside the shop for a second and when he came out, he was gone.

'Which shop was that sir?'

'Look, we need to get back there, in case the man at the shop has found him,' Jack said, and with that, turned on his heels and started running back towards the corner shop with the officer in pursuit.

As he approached the shop, the man was standing at the door looking up the promenade towards him, shrugging his shoulders with hands outstretched, indicating his lack of success. Now Jack was distraught; with every second that ticked by, whoever had taken Toby would be further away and the chance of finding him was diminishing.

The officer now took charge. Opening her note-book, she forced Jack to concentrate by asking him questions about Toby and the pushchair. How old is he? What kind of pushchair is it? What colour is it?

'Look, I need to be looking for him, not standing here doing nothing!' Jack suddenly shouted, feeling that she was wasting precious time.

'Alright sir,' she said, 'Look, the quickest way to find your son is to let the police know he's missing.'

With that, she took out her mobile phone and rang the station, putting them in the picture and giving them the details Jack had provided.

'Come with me now, to the station, where we'll be able to wait for news. We have people all over the town and I'm sure he'll be spotted soon. Where is your wife? Was she with you?'

At the mention of his wife, Jack's legs buckled, and he nearly fell to the ground.

'Oh my god! Grace!' he said with renewed horror in his voice. 'She'll be expecting us! What can I do? I...I...I can't tell her!'

'Well, she will obviously have to be told. We'll call her from the station. There may be some news by then.'

***

There was no news. The sergeant had rung Grace and she had taken a taxi to the police station. She was standing by the counter as Jack and the PSO walked in. She immediately screamed at him,

'You idiot! What have you done! Where is my son! I knew I shouldn't have let you take him!'

Jack seemed to visibly shrink, and mumbled 'Grace, I ... I... ,'

'Don't you dare say 'Sorry'!' she shouted. The police sergeant intervened at this point saying,

'Look, I know this is horrendous for you both, but this isn't helping. We're doing all we can to find him, and you know, people do usually turn up safe and sound.'

'What? You expect a two-year-old boy to come walking in here when he's had enough of his adventure? Don't be ridiculous!' Grace exclaimed. 'Whoever has taken him isn't likely to bring him back either, are they?'

At this, Grace collapsed in tears. Jack tried to put his arms round her to comfort her, but she pushed him away declaring,

'Get away from me! If anything happens to Toby, I'll kill you!'

Everyone could see that, at that moment, she absolutely meant it!

A young policewoman quickly ushered them into a room and asked them to take a seat. Sitting down across the table from them, she took out a notebook and asked Jack to describe exactly what had happened. This incensed him. It was obvious, he half shouted; his son had been stolen! Why weren't they out there looking for him. There was no time for all this. With every minute that passed Toby was being taken further away from them.

The policewoman assured him there were dozens of officers scouring the town at that very moment. The best thing he could do was tell her exactly what had happened. Had he seen anyone observing them when he and Toby were on the beach? Had he noticed anyone watching them, either earlier in the day or as he was walking across the road to the convenience store?

Jack shook his head and buried his face in his hands, saying,

'Oh God, what a nightmare!!'

Grace could contain herself no longer and launched another verbal attack on Jack.

'For God's sake Jack! You must have seen someone – think man!' she screamed at him.

The policewoman intervened,

'I know this is horrendous for you Mrs Long, but please, try to calm down. Shouting at your husband is not helpful right now. We need to help him remember every detail of what happened.'

Grace sat back and nodded.

'Yes, of course, I'm sorry,' she agreed.

The policewoman tried once more to focus Jack's mind. She needed to glean any information she could; anything that may give them a clue as to what had happened to the little boy.

'We are, of course, questioning everyone in the vicinity – the stall holders and shopkeepers and so on, but if there's anything, however small, that you can remember, now's the time to tell us, Mr Long.'

Jack was silent, obviously trying hard to remember if he'd seen anything that had struck him as odd while they were on the beach. Suddenly, he looked up and exclaimed,

'Yes! There was a young woman sitting nearby. She grabbed Toby when he tried to run off with his spade. I thought she was just helping me, but now – I'm not so sure!'

'Can you describe this woman, Mr Long? How old was she, do you think? What colour hair had she and how was she dressed?'

Jack proceeded to give what details he could. Although he now remembered she had been around for quite a while, until Toby had run off, he hadn't taken much notice of her. Anyway, he did his best and gave them what he thought was a reasonable description of her. She was in her early twenties, he felt, with blond hair. She was wearing pink shorts and a white top and had some sort of trainers on her feet; he would be able to recognise if he saw her again.

The policewoman seemed relieved that at last Jack had given them something to go on, and left the room, presumably to pass on the information, saying she would be back shortly, and would they like a cup of tea.

Jack tried once more to comfort his wife, but she pushed him away again, saying

'Get away from me! Toby's gone – I'll never forgive you for this!'

'But Grace, I swear I only took my eyes off him for a split second! Whoever took him must have been right there outside that shop. Someone must have seen them take him!'

For the rest of the day the police searched all over the town, and checked the bus and railway station CC TV cameras. There was no sign of Toby. Jack and Grace were beside themselves. Grace's anger gave way to abject fear. Five years of her life had been dominated with her desire for a child and when Toby had finally come along it was like a miracle. He became her sole reason for living and the thought that she might have lost him filled her with terror, but also with a visceral hatred of her husband.

The police put notices out around the town showing a photo of Toby, and the local television station put it on the news. Jack and Grace were asked to do a press conference appealing for information and for the person who had taken him to bring him home. Jack could barely speak. He was consumed with guilt, constantly asking himself how could he have allowed this to happen to his son, and he knew that every person watching would have been asking the same question. What kind of a father was he? Grace didn't make it any easier for him, and it was obvious to anyone who watched them that she blamed her husband for the loss of their son.

A few people came forward with sightings, which the police followed up, but none of them came to anything. One week, two weeks, eventually a month went by, and Grace began to realise she may never see Toby again. She never spoke to Jack now. She couldn't even look at him. He was hardly ever at home anyway. When he wasn't working, he was walking the town in search of his son. He refused to stop, unable to accept what had happened.

As the months passed, Grace sank into a depression. She never went out, sometimes didn't even get out of bed. Each morning when she woke, she had to remember all over again that her little boy was gone and with each remembering she sank deeper into despair. Then one day, when Jack came home from another day of searching, he found her in the bath with her wrists slashed. In an utter panic he rang for an ambulance, but he knew that it was too late. She was gone.

Of course, he blamed himself for her death. If he hadn't allowed someone to take his son, if he'd been a better father, Grace would never have done anything like this. In spite of the way they had drifted apart since Toby was born, they had loved each other very much once, and he had hoped that if ever they were able to get over their loss, they might do so again.

Now he could see it had been hopeless to ever think that. Losing her son had destroyed Grace and it was his fault. She would never have forgiven him.

The next days passed by in a haze. As he had discovered her body, the police inevitably interviewed him at length, until they were satisfied that Grace had indeed committed suicide. He couldn't function and Grace's brother took control of the funeral arrangements. People were very kind. No one blamed him even though he blamed himself. He felt that his life was over too.

Chapter One

Jack felt the sudden rocking of the boat and opened his eyes to see the reflection of sunlight on the water playing on the ceiling of his narrowboat. Some idiot trying to break the water speed record, probably one of those light, fast fibreglass jobs. They don't show any concern for the effect they have on the rest of us, he thought to himself. Ben, his chocolate lab, lifted his head, stretched, and lumbered to his feet. Padding over to Jack he licked his face in greeting.

'Okay, okay, I know, just hang on a minute.'

Since he'd been living on the boat Ben had been Jack's only companion. They were inseparable and he made Jack's isolation from the rest of the world bearable. He climbed out of bed and opened the double doors at the end of the cabin. Swilling his face in the sink he quickly threw on his jeans and tee-shirt, then up on deck, positioned the plank across the gap between the boat and the bank and led Ben into the

1

woods at the other side of the towpath for the dog to relieve itself. It was a bright morning, the haze hanging over the canal promising it would be a hot one, once the sun had dried up the mist.

Back on the boat, Jack finished getting dressed and soon the smell of frying bacon pervaded the space. Not a bad life, he thought to himself as he ate his sandwich. Ben sat at his feet looking up expectantly, waiting for the scrap his master invariably gave him. Jack smiled down at his friend as he sat, motionless, head up, eyes fixed on Jack's.

'Okay, wait for it!' he said, then gave him the last of his breakfast before getting up to give him his tin of 'Chappie' and fill his water bowl.

Jack glanced at his watch. Time to be getting a move on, he told himself. He needed to get down to the Job Centre to sign on, as he had to do every week, if he wanted to keep receiving his benefit payment. It was his main source of income nowadays, so he couldn't afford to miss his appointment. They would ask him the same question they always did, how many jobs had he applied for and had he been given any interviews. His answer was invariably the same. He had applied for several jobs as he did every week, but without gaining one interview. At nearly forty-five years old, without current qualifications and with a drink driving conviction, he, and they, knew he didn't stand much of a chance.

He had worked for many years as a delivery driver for the Post Office until a stupid mistake caused him to lose his driving job, along with any chance of getting another. For years, after the dual tragedy of losing his son and his wife's suicide, he'd struggled with his mental health. He suffered from vivid flashbacks to those dreadful events. The only thing that helped then was alcohol, although he had made it a rule not to let his drinking affect his work. He'd been having a particularly hard day and had stupidly stopped to get himself a bottle of whiskey to take home. Not content with that, he took off the top and took a swig, and then another, and before he knew it, he'd drunk several. He knew he shouldn't drive but he had to get the van back for the next delivery round.

On the way back to the depot, the inevitable happened. A kid ran across in front of him and he stamped on the brakes, resulting in the car behind shunting into the back of the van. The lad ran off, thankfully unhurt, but the driver had suffered a bump on the head and insisted on calling the police. When the policeman was interviewing Jack, he inevitably smelt the whiskey and saw the bottle on the passenger seat. He was breathalysed and was way over the limit. Arrested and charged with drink driving, he was dismissed from his job, fined, banned for two years and given 100 hours of community service.

Realising he would struggle to get work, given his record, and with no ties or responsibilities, he decided to sell up and buy a narrow boat. He'd answered a classified ad for one in the Canal Boat magazine. The Lady Louise turned out to be just what he needed. She was a fifty-foot traditional narrowboat with everything a man could need to live comfortably.

That was seven years ago now and he'd never worked since. He still suffered from flashbacks of the day Toby was taken, and the day he found his wife dead in the bath, but no longer used alcohol to forget. For one thing, he couldn't afford it, but for another, he'd found a different way to deal with the memories. He had taken up painting the wildlife along the banks of the canal. He found that once he was absorbed in creating a painting, he could forget everything else completely, and this is how he got through his days. The nights, of course, were not so easy. Each weekend he took the boat along the canal and through the lock to an area where several artists and potters lined their boats up to sell their wares to the tourists. He didn't make much money, but it subsidised his benefits and allowed him to pay the mooring fees, river license and fuel for the boat.

He had left Ben in the boat as they wouldn't permit dogs in the Job Centre and now, as he walked down into the town, he was thinking that it wasn't such a bad life he'd carved out for himself, given what had happened. He had enough to eat, enjoyed being on the boat and, particularly in the summer, it was pleasant enough. The winter wasn't so great of course, but with his woodstove going most of the time he managed to keep warm. With no tourists to buy his paintings he spent his time building up his stock for when they returned in the spring.

It was a solitary existence, but he had Ben for company, and it suited him. He had no desire to get into conversation with anyone beyond the occasional 'Hello'. He lived in fear of anyone asking him about himself, where he had come from, why he was living on a narrowboat - anything at all really, and so he kept to himself. That was just how he liked it. There had been the odd person over the years who had tried to befriend him, but he had always managed to put them off, even being rude when they didn't take the hint.

When he arrived at the Job Centre, he took his ticket and sat down to wait. When his turn came, he strode over to the window and gave the young woman his name and National Insurance number. The girl hardly looked old enough to be working. However, she had obviously been well trained in dealing with people here for handouts. She barely raised her head to look Jack in the eye. She just mumbled the usual questions whilst looking down at the counter, which made Jack feel like asserting that actually, he was a human being who surely qualified for a certain level of courtesy. Of course, he said nothing. He had long since realised it was pointless demanding to be treated as anything other than a number. You couldn't fight the system.

After he'd signed on, he checked out the available jobs on the noticeboard, making a note on his phone of a few that looked remotely promising. He had no expectation of getting any of them, but he knew he had to play the game if he wanted to eat. He intended to go through the weekly routine of submitting applications for some of them using his phone when he got back to the boat.

He stopped at the cash machine on the way back, calling in at the corner shop to stock up with what he would need for the coming week. As he approached the boat, he could hear Ben jumping about and barking, making a fuss as he always did when he heard Jack coming. As he opened the doors, the dog jumped up at him, excitedly licking his face.

'Alright old boy!' Jack declared. 'Goodness, I've only been gone an hour! You'd think I'd been away for a week, the way you go on.'

Eventually, Ben calmed down and Jack made himself a cup of tea, then settled down on the rear deck with Ben at his feet and took out his phone to carry out the weekly trawl through the situations vacant. He found a couple of warehousing jobs he could apply for online, carefully saving the details in the file named 'job applications' in his phone, to satisfy the 'jobsworth' at the Job Centre.

He decided to do some painting. Taking out his easel and paintbox he settled down to paint the image of a kingfisher on a branch that he'd managed to capture on his phone the previous week. Ben was sitting on the bench opposite him, watching the squirrels jumping about in the trees along the towpath. Jack had just about managed to lose himself in his painting when he heard a cycle bell in the distance. He glanced up and noticed a boy coming towards him along the path. Ben's ears went up and he sat upright on the bench.

Jack glanced at the boy. He looked about eleven or twelve and was riding a mountain bike.

The boy stopped beside the boat, and jumped off his bike, but said nothing at first. He was looking at Ben who was now standing, wagging his tail and watching at the boy expectantly, waiting for a reaction.

'Hello,' the boy ventured.

Reluctantly Jack looked up from his work.

'Hello,' he said briskly.

'What's your dog called, Mister?' the boy asked shyly.

'None of your business,' Jack replied, eager not to encourage further interaction with the lad. However, he couldn't help feeling sorry as he watched the boy's face collapse in disappointment. Ignoring his own feelings, however, he lowered his head and carried on with his painting. For a full minute, the lad stood there, staring at Ben who, in spite of his master's attitude, still looked eager for contact with him. Finally, he climbed back on his bike and rode off along the canal path.

This short encounter had caused an unexpected reaction in Jack. The boy was about the same age Toby would have been if only ... The sight of the lad's blond curls awakened a precious memory; the feel of Toby's beneath his fingers when he ruffled his hair affectionately, as he invariably did as he left for work. Once again, he was filled with feelings of guilt and regret. Would he never find release from the torment of these memories?

Chapter Two

Detective Chief Inspector Alex Scott pulled up outside the neat, detached house in Wavertree Avenue. The events of the day had disturbed her greatly. A young girl, Holly Davenport, no older than her own daughter, Aby, had been found dead by her father. It appeared she had committed suicide by taking an overdose of her mother's sleeping tablets. Alex shook her head in an attempt to remove the image of the child lying there, with her lifeless eyes staring into infinity.

Dragging herself back to the present, she sat for a few moments staring at the house. Whatever else was going on in her life, or her job, Alex was always proud of her home and family. She and Dave had done well. It had been a stretch in the early years. They had bought the house off-plan, a new build which had really been just a shell. Gradually they had made it their own. Aby and Johnny had been born and grown up here. It was now her refuge from everything. Being in the force could be very stressful and it was sometimes difficult not to bring it home with her, but she always did her best.

As she opened the front door and stepped into her own private world, she could hear the kids bickering over something or nothing as usual, and the sound of Dave pottering about in the kitchen. She smiled to herself and walked through into the kitchen. The radio was playing, and Dave was busy preparing vegetables at the sink as she snook up behind him, sliding her arms around his waist. He jumped, then gasped,

'Oh my God, you startled me,' then went on to say, 'come here Mrs Scott. How dare you take advantage of a chap peeling potatoes! Is there no respect anywhere?'

For a long luxurious moment they embraced, then enjoyed a lingering kiss before Alex pulled away saying,

'I need a shower! It's been a stressful day. I can't be very pleasant to be around.'

'Oh! That's what that awful smell is!' Dave joked, laughingly, 'Off you go then, dinner'll be in half an hour.'

Alex enjoyed a hot shower, feeling herself relax as she pushed away the memories of the day's events. By the time she had dried her hair and pulled on her joggers and top, Dave was calling up the stairs to summon the family to the supper table. As she emerged from the bedroom, Johnny and Aby were competing for access to the staircase.

'For goodness sake, you two, can't you ever agree on anything?'

'Oh, hi mum!' Johnny exclaimed, then stopped in his tracks and holding his sister back, gave an exaggerated bow, and sweeping his left arm, gestured for his mother to lead them down the stairs.

Sitting round the table in the dining room Alex looked across at her children. She was proud of them both, even though they could be excruciatingly annoying at times, particularly with their constant bickering.

'So, how was your day, you two?' she asked.

'OK thanks mum,' Johnny replied. 'We had a great chemistry class today – lots of fire and explosions!' adding with a twinkle in his eye, 'I might try some of them at home with that chemistry set grandma bought me.'

'Yeah, right!' his sister declared. 'You'd probably burn the house down!'

'Yes, best leave that sort of thing to the experts,' David interjected.

'What about you Aby, what've you been up to today?'

'Every time I looked, she was on her phone,' her brother helpfully explained.

'No, I wasn't,' she said defensively.

Alex looked at her daughter who was looking down at her plate, avoiding her mother's gaze. A knot of fear suddenly gripped Alex and the image of the young girl reasserted itself in her mind. She made a mental note to keep a closer eye on the way Aby. They had finally given in to her demands for a mobile phone about six months ago. In many ways it made sense for her to have one. At least they could always reach her and with the tracker app, could even know exactly where she was. But of course, where she went to online was another matter, and that's where danger lurked. Alex knew that only too well. There was already some evidence that the youngster who had died that day had been using her phone to access material about suicide that was totally inappropriate for anyone, let alone a young, impressionable teenager to see.

Of course, Alex knew that this wasn't the time to talk to Aby about it, and to lighten her own mood as much as anything else, she told them that she had been thinking it was time they went down to Tidmouth to visit grandma and grandad. This created much excitement, and it was agreed that they should go at half term, as both Alex and Dave had already booked a week's holiday off work then. Alex promised to ring her mother later to check they would be happy for them to go, not that there was much doubt about that. They were always happy to see the children and make a fuss of them.

Over the next few weeks Alex and her team investigated Holly's death and concluded that she had indeed, tragically, taken her own life. There was of course a postmortem followed by the Coroner's Inquest. There were other cases for Alex to deal with, but this one was particularly harrowing given the echoes of the concerns she had for her own daughter. She had found dealing with the anguish of Holly's parents particularly affecting as she tried to maintain a professional distance, but it was all too easy to identify with how they were feeling.

Chapter Three

It was a couple of weeks later that the boy turned up at the boat again. Jack was working on the roof, stacking the logs he'd been chopping to build up his supply of fuel for his stove. Ben was sitting on the grass at the side of the towpath when he saw the boy approaching and jumping up, barked his greeting. The lad hopped off his bike and began to make a fuss of Ben.

'Ben!' shouted Jack, 'Come here boy!'

Ben stopped, looked first at the lad and then at Jack, then trotting back aboard the boat, jumpedg up onto the roof beside his master. Jack looked at the lad, who once again was looking hurt that he hadn't been allowed to interact with Ben.

'I only wanted to stroke him,' he said quietly. 'I'm Archie by the way.'

'Well,' Jack replied, 'I don't allow anyone to get involved with my dog, so don't get any ideas about making friends with him. Now, I'll thank you to get on your way.'

***

With that, Archie said nothing, he just climbed on his bike and rode back the way he had come. He couldn't understand why the man on the boat had stopped him from stroking his dog, which had obviously been eager for contact with him. As he rode his bike towards home, he wondered why the man so obviously didn't like him. Otherwise, he would have been happy to let him fuss the dog. Grownups can be so confusing he thought, as he lifted the latch and pushed his bike through the gate.

The back door was open, and his mother was busy making lunch.

'Oh, I'm glad you're back Archie, lunch is nearly ready. Go and wash your hands now.'

'What is for lunch, Mum?' Archie asked.

'Your favourite, burgers in a bap,' she replied.

'Great,' he declared and then, realising just how hungry he was after his bike ride, hurried up to the bathroom.

As they were sitting eating lunch at the small table in the kitchen, Archie said,

'I saw a great dog today, Mum.'

'That's nice love,' his mum replied, not really paying much attention, as she was writing out her shopping list for her trip to the supermarket that afternoon.

'It was funny though. It was a friendly dog and wanted me to stroke it, but the man on the boat said I couldn't, and told me to go away. That wasn't nice, was it mum?'

Mum carried on writing her list.

'Mum! That wasn't very nice, was it?' Archie insisted.

'What wasn't?' Mum asked absently.

'Mum, you're not listening to me!'

At that, his mother put down her pen and turned her attention to her son.

'I'm sorry love, tell me again, what wasn't very nice?'

Archie gave a huge sigh but then started again and told her about his encounter with the dog.

'Well, maybe the dog could be a bit unpredictable and that's why he didn't want you to touch it,' his mother suggested.

'Well, it didn't look unpredictable to me, and why was he so rude, telling me to go away?'

'Where was this, Archie?'

'On the canal,' he replied.

Archie now had his mum's full attention.

'I've told you before, I don't want you riding along the canal path, haven't I? I just don't feel it's safe for you to go along there on your own!' she said with some force.

'But mum, it's just made for riding a bike! I don't understand why you don't want me to.'

'Because, my lad, you just never know who you might meet. Take this chap with the dog, he didn't seem very friendly, did he?'

'Well, no he didn't, but I wasn't in any danger, was I?'

'Probably not, but you never know, so I don't want you taking the risk. Look, I tell you what, why don't we both take a ride along there at the weekend? Maybe if he's still there I can get to meet this dog of yours, and his owner too. Then I can see for myself. How's that?'

Archie reluctantly agreed. In any case it would be fun to take a ride with his mum, he was missing the friends he'd left behind at their old place. For her part Alice was relieved Archie seemed to accept this suggestion. She was aware she was probably over-protective of him. He was all she had after all. She knew he was growing up fast and it terrified her. Soon he would grow away from her, becoming a person in his own right. She also knew there would be questions. Questions she could never answer, and she had no idea how she would handle that. She'd noticed that he had become increasingly attracted to spending time with older men, presumably because he was subconsciously looking for the father he'd never known.

Indeed, that's why they had recently moved here. He had been getting far too attached to a neighbour living two doors down and Alice felt the man was taking an unhealthy interest in her son. As a single parent she'd never been in a position to buy a house, but her teacher's salary had allowed her to rent a reasonable property in the nearby town where they had lived for some years. So now it had been relatively easy to find a decent place here, and this semi-detached house just south of the town centre suited her and Archie very well. As he would have been changing school anyway in September, she had sorted out a place for him at St Cuthbert's School in the town.

So, the last thing Alice wanted was for Archie to get involved with this man who lived on a narrowboat. Of course, she reasoned, perhaps she needn't worry as the man and his dog would more than likely be moving on anyway, given the itinerant life he was apparently leading. She was hoping that when they took their bike ride next Saturday, he would have gone on his way, and that would be the last she would hear of him.

As she cleared away the dishes, Alice neatly diverted Archie's mind away from the subject of the canal and its residents, asking him to sort out the bags for their trip to the supermarket. As a twelve-year-old, he was still happy to go with her on her shopping trips, always with an eye on any special offers on the video games shelf that he might persuade his mum to buy or rent for him.

Chapter Four

The second visit from the boy had left Jack in a strange mood. He felt annoyed at the intrusion into his solitary existence, dragging to the surface memories he had learned to bury over the years, simply by never engaging in any meaningful way with another human being. However, the sight of the lad had awakened something in his heart he had thought had gone forever, and it terrified him. The boy must live somewhere nearby and obviously liked to ride his bike along the towpath. Jack suspected he would be back again before too long. Maybe it was time to move on. Of course, he couldn't leave the area completely because of his weekly visits to the Jobcentre, but he could move to the other side of the town, a distance he judged would be too far for the boy to venture.

By early afternoon he was packed up and ready to move off. He took Ben for his last trip to the woods, then untied the mooring rope. Back on the boat he stowed the gangplank, and they were ready. Ben knew the signs and was excited. He jumped up onto the seat at the side of the cockpit beside Jack at the rear of the boat, ears pricked, ready for the next adventure.

'Okay boy,' Jack murmured, 'let's be on our way.'

He turned the ignition, and the engine threw out a blue haze as it stuttered into life. Then, as he pushed the gear lever forward, he eased the Lady Louise away from the bank and into the middle of the canal. The afternoon was warm with hardly a cloud in the sky. He noticed a water vole swimming across the canal ahead of him, and a family of moorhens scurried out of his way, their heads bobbing back and forth, which always made him smile. In fact, the sights and sounds of the wildlife along the banks soothed Jack's mood and he began to look forward to a change of scene.

To reach the north side of the town would mean navigating the lock which lay about a mile further on. Jack was hoping it wouldn't be too busy, although it would be helpful if there was at least one other boat waiting to go through. It was difficult enough to deal with the business of passing through a lock alone. It would also be helpful if the lock was full of water, meaning that he could sail straight in. The whole pro-cedure could take as much as twenty minutes, but rather less if he had the help of another boat owner.

As he rounded the last bend before starting on the straight quarter mile or so before the lock, he could see there were in fact several boats tied up along the towpath, but apparently none of them were waiting to go through the lock. Then he was pleased to see the lock gates being opened, as a boat arrived from the lower level. He made his way at full throttle towards the gates, indicating to the woman steering the boat out of the lock that he would be entering it. The man who was getting ready to close the gates after the boat had passed through, waved to him to indicate he would leave the gates open for him.

After navigating the lock without incident, Jack could see another boat waiting to pass through in the opposite direction, so on this occasion he didn't need to bother closing the gates and was able to sail on. After a mile or so, he found a suitable mooring and pulled into the bank. The canal here was high, the woods falling sharply away towards the river flowing along the valley floor. On the opposite side of the canal, the land rose steeply towards the road running high along the hillside. It wasn't as convenient for Ben as his previous mooring, but it would be fine for the moment. Maybe in a few weeks he would be able to move back again, once the boy had given up looking for him. Now he was annoyed with himself for allowing thoughts of the boy to return. What was wrong with him, he wondered?

Over the next few weeks Jack busied himself painting pictures for the tourists. There was plenty of material around and he captured as many images as he could on his phone. Early mornings were best, with the heat haze often hovering over the canal. He had no need of an alarm clock as the dawn chorus started up at around five o'clock. Often, he would get up and sit quietly on the deck, ready to photograph anything that moved. Then he would climb onto the towpath to take a few views of the valley and the hillside beyond the river. By now Ben had usually woken up and joined him, gazing up at him expectantly, pleading for his breakfast.

One particularly beautiful morning he had been sitting quietly gazing into the woods on the other side of the canal when a young deer suddenly appeared in the undergrowth and for one magical moment stood stock still, looking directly into his eyes. He was transfixed, and before he could capture the image, the deer turned and was gone. It was only a moment, and even though he hadn't managed to record it on his phone, the image was imprinted on his brain, and he would never forget it. It was a picture he captured in paint more than once over the years that followed, always marvelling how such an encounter with a wild creature could remain fixed so vividly in his memory.

Chapter Five

As Alice had promised, on the Saturday after Archie's second encounter with Jack and Ben, they had taken their ride along the towpath. To Archie's disappointment, neither Ben nor the boat were anywhere to be seen.

'Never mind Archie,' Alice said, 'people living on the boats move around a lot. They've probably moved on along the canal now, so perhaps it's best just to forget about it.'

'I'll try Mum, but I really liked Ben,' Archie had replied sadly.

'I know love,' she went on. 'Look, how will it be if we look into getting you a dog of your own?'

'Mum!! Do you really mean it? Can I really have my own dog?'

'I don't see why not Archie, let's see what we can do.'

Archie was delighted. His own dog! At this, thoughts of Ben subsided, and he began to comb the Internet looking at breeds of dog, wondering what kind his mum would suggest. She said it would have to be a rescue dog as she couldn't afford to buy a particular breed. She would also have to check with the landlord, as some didn't like tenants keeping pets.

It was some weeks later that Alice finally had word from the landlord saying that he wouldn't mind them having a dog, as long as it was short-haired and didn't become a nuisance to the neighbours. Alice contacted the dog rescue centre, and added her name to the waiting list, specifying that the dog must be short-haired and able to be handled by a twelve-year-old boy. A month later she received a call to say they had what they thought would be a perfect dog for them. It was a blond Labrador, about two years old, and although not a small dog, it was gentle and would, they thought, make the perfect companion for a twelve-year-old boy. Apparently, it had been well treated and was in the rescue centre because, sadly, its elderly owner had recently passed away. When Alice told Archie he was thrilled and couldn't wait for the weekend, when they would be able to go along to meet her. As soon as he set eyes on her, Archie's heart was lost. She looked up at him with her gentle, black eyes, and he knew; this was to be his dog!

A few days later, once the paperwork and the injections had been dealt with, Alice and Archie returned to collect Trixie. Alice had managed to find a cage for her on Gumtree so that she would be kept secure when they had to leave her alone, and it didn't take long for her to settle in, seemingly quite content with the arrangement. Of course, whenever Archie was at home, they were inseparable, and Trixie was soon trotting along happily beside him whenever he went out on his bike. Alice felt much easier letting him roam a little with Trixie beside him, and he resumed his rides along the towpath, until the cold and wet of autumn put a temporary stop to that.

***

Archie had started at his new school in the second week of September. It had seemed strange because not only did he know no-one, he was also one of the youngest in the school and he found it rather daunting. He didn't know where anything was, or what was expected of him. On the other hand, the lessons were more interesting, and he was soon learning about Kings and Queens of old, and where England sat in the world, what the world was made of, and lots of other interesting things. He was a bright lad and couldn't get enough information, soaking up everything like a sponge.

Alice was getting to grips with her new year group. She had been given a year 7 tutor group who were quite a handful. Many of them had come from the more deprived end of town and were ill-prepared for secondary school. It was always a challenge though at the start of the year, Alice mused, as she surveyed her charges.

As for her maths students, as always she tried to assess which ones would be receptive to learning, and which ones would need more encouragement. It was difficult to balance the two. It was important to Alice to nurture the more talented so that they could reach their full potential. At the same time, she was determined to help less motivated students to raise their expectations. It would have been all too easy for her, with one eye on the league tables, to accept their belief they would never achieve anything academically, and to just concentrate on maximising the successes of the brighter children. Alice, however, genuinely believed that every pupil deserved the best education the school could provide.

Someone else had grabbed Alice's attention though. At the first assembly of the year, the headmistress Mrs Gloucester, had introduced a new member of staff. Samantha Bolton had been recruited to teach science and Alice was intrigued. She was probably about thirty, with short, curly hair and a face that looked as though it knew exactly where it was going. There was an energy and strength about her that drew Alice's admiration before she had even spoken to her.

The strength of the attraction Alice was feeling was disconcerting. She'd never had a close relationship with a man. She had had friends who were men of course, but she had only become intimate with one of them and didn't really count the juvenile fumblings of a couple of sixteen-year-olds twelve years before, as a relationship, even though it had very unexpected and far-reaching consequences. This was something she had never talked about to anyone, if she had, how would she explain about Archie? That's not to say she had never felt any stirrings of desire. The first time was with Miss Longley, the gym teacher at school with whom she became deeply infatuated. Afterwards she had attributed this to a schoolgirl crush. Then later on there was Sal at college. She was a bright young woman with a ready smile that captivated Alice from the start. She now began to realise that she was definitely more attracted to women than men, and when it became apparent that Sal was actually only interested in flirting with any passing male, Alice forced herself to concentrate on her studies. In any case, she had Archie to look after and had neither time nor energy to seek special friendships. So, as the years went on, her conviction grew that she was gay, although she had never done anything about it. She supposed that was because the opportunity had never arisen.

However, now, at the age of twenty-eight, the arrival of Samantha Bolton had once again awoken those flutterings of desire in the pit of her stomach. She found herself seizing every opportunity to be near her. To her delight, Alice found that whenever they had the chance of a one-to-one conversation, Sam seemed only too happy to chatter on, and seemed equally interested to listen to whatever she had to say. It turned out she was unmarried and in fact without a partner. She had only just arrived in the area and was renting a flat in town until, she said, she could find a little house to buy. As the weeks passed, the signals between them grew stronger. Eye contacts lasted a little too long producing an exquisite yearning in

Alice, and she longed to tell Sam how she was feeling. However, she was still unsure of her.

The half term break was approaching, and Alice and Sam found themselves the last to leave the staff room as the school day drew to a close. Neither seemed keen to leave, both of them shuffling papers around and trying not to look each other in the eye. Finally, Sam declared,

'Look, this is ridiculous!'

Alice looked up sharply, heart pounding, anticipating what she was going to say.

'Can we go out for a meal or something? I mean, if that's what you'd like, or we could take in a film, or just go to the pub...' she gabbled on.

'Yes, please,' Alice interjected, rather too quickly she thought, but it was too late now.

They both smiled, relieved that their journey together had finally begun.

Then, remembering Archie, Alice said,

'I would love to, really, but I have a son, Archie, and he's too young to be left alone. I don't have a regular babysitter either, as it's not long since we moved into the town.'

Sam looked a little taken aback, wondering whether she'd misread the signs, as Alice had a son, but nevertheless went on,

'No problem,' she said, 'let's all do something together.'

'If you're sure you don't mind,' Alice replied. 'What were you thinking of?'

'Well, I believe there's a Safari Park somewhere near here, do you think he'd like that?'

'I should say so, he's been pestering me for months to take him there.'

'That's settled then. It's half-term the week after next, why don't we go then?'

So, it was agreed that they would go on the first Monday of the half term holiday. Alice was excited. She had never felt like this before. She longed to spend time with Sam and could think of little else. In fact, she became quite annoyed with herself, telling herself not to be so childishly impatient. She was feeling like a lovesick schoolgirl, and she just hoped she wasn't showing it.

Chapter Six

It was on the Friday before half term that Alice told Archie she had a treat planned for him. They were to visit the Safari Park, and would be going with Sam, the new science teacher at her school. Archie didn't know what to make of this. Until now, it had always been just himself and his mum. They didn't need anyone else, did they? All he needed was Trixie and his mum. And why were they going to the Safari Park? He'd asked her many times before and she'd always said it was too expensive, and now suddenly, presumably because this Sam had suggested it, it was fine. Not only that, but he also wouldn't even be able to take Trixie.

So it was with some apprehension that he woke on the Monday morning, realising it was the day he was to meet this Sam. Even the fact they were going to the Safari Park did nothing to make him feel better about it. Alice had put out some new jeans and sweatshirt for him to wear and made sure he took a shower. These were all bad signs. He felt as if he were being groomed specially to meet this person. By the time the strange car, a white golf estate, pulled up outside at 10 am, Archie was totally convinced that he didn't like the driver even though he had never yet set eyes on him.

He noticed his mum was wearing a bright yellow dress he'd never seen before and seemed excited as she opened the door.

'Hi,' she exclaimed, 'do come in!'

Archie was hanging back, holding on to Trixie who sometimes got nervous when confronted with someone new.

'This is my son, Archie,' Alice said, as she invited Sam into the living room.

'Hi Archie,' Sam said, 'It's great to meet you.'

Archie was shocked. Sam was a woman! He had rather assumed his mum's friend would be a man. After a second or two he replied with a guarded 'Hello'.

'And who is this?' Sam asked, bending down and offering her hand for Trixie to sniff.

Trixie promptly started to lick Sam's hand and Archie's attitude softened immediately.

'She's my dog, Trixie,' he replied.

'She's lovely,' Sam asserted.

'Shall we have a cuppa, or would you rather get off?' Alice asked, speaking to neither of them in particular.

As one, both Sam and Archie quickly confirmed that they wanted to go straight away.

Alice smiled and said,

'Right then, let's go!' pleased that this first

encounter between these two important people in her life had gone so well.

Archie coaxed Trixie into her cage and settled her down on her cushion before following Sam out to her car. Alice locked up and followed them, feeling happier than she had done for some time. It was going to be a great day, she was sure.

Sam insisted on taking them in her car, which suited Alice very well. Archie was impressed, this was a VW Golf estate, far superior in his mind, to his mother's red escort. He clambered into the back, and Alice sat in the front. Sam was obviously an accomplished driver, using the power the car had in reserve whenever it was safe to do so, which Archie found exciting.

'Shall we have some music?' Sam asked.

'Sure, why not,' Alice replied.

Soon they were all singing along to Adele. This was a wholly new experience for both Archie and Alice and with every mile the day promised to be one to remember, and so it proved to be. The Safari Park was every bit as exciting as Archie had long imagined, particularly the lions, as they lumbered past the car, eyeball to eyeball! The monkeys were hilarious, clambering all over the tops of the cars and peering into the windscreens, chattering loudly.

They had lunch in the cafe and Archie was allowed his favourite, burger with fries, while Sam and Alice enjoyed pizza and salad. The afternoon was spent wandering around the rest of the animal enclosures.

Archie had to admit to himself that Sam didn't seem too bad. In fact, she was fun, and also generous, paying for the lunch and the ice-creams they enjoyed later on.

However, he also noticed that his mother kept looking at her in a funny way which somehow made Archie a bit nervous. In fact, a few times when he'd spoken to his mum, her attention had been on Sam, and she'd completely ignored him. This was definitely something new. He several times had to tug at her sleeve to get her attention which, to his dismay, made her cross and she had snapped at him, telling him to wait a moment as she was listening to Sam, or not to be rude, interrupting their conversation. This was not a reaction he was used to, and it made him feel very uncomfortable indeed. He had no idea how to deal with this emotion, as he had never felt it before. He couldn't even put a name to it.

Apart from that, the day went well and passed by all too quickly. When they arrived back at the house Alice invited Sam in for a drink, but to her dismay she declined, saying she had a few things to do that evening, but didn't specify what they were. Alice was filled with doubt after she'd gone. Perhaps she hadn't enjoyed the day after all. Maybe it had been a mistake to suggest that their first 'date' had to include Archie. After all, a twelve-year-old boy can be rather trying, and Archie had been pestering her for attention more than usual all day.

***

In fact Sam had enjoyed the day immensely but had hoped that Alice would have been more forthcoming regarding Archie. Had she been in a relationship with his dad, in which case, had she got this all wrong? She had been attracted to Alice from the moment they'd met on her first morning at the school, and she had been sure that her feelings were reciprocated. Now she wasn't so sure and that's why she had felt the need to get away, she would have to hold back from saying anything to Alice about how she felt until she was more sure about her.

***

For his part, although Archie had enjoyed the Safari Park, he certainly had not been too happy to share his mother's attention, even with Sam, who he had to admit seemed nice enough. So, he was cross with his mum, not with Sam. Trixie was excited to be released from her cage and Archie took her out for a walk in the nearby woods. There was a pond a little way in, and he spent some time skimming stones while Trixie had a swim. Then he sat down on a nearby tree stump and reflected on the day, trying to make sense of the way he was feeling. It was very confusing.

Although he had initially resented the idea of his mum having a special friend, a small part of him had often wondered whether it might be fun if she had a boyfriend. He missed having a man in his life, particularly when he saw his friends playing footie with theirs. As he sat there throwing sticks for Trixie to retrieve, the thought that had often drifted into his mind, now reappeared. Why didn't he have a dad? He knew that of course, he must have had one once, but he had never known him and whenever he asked his mum about it, she told him not to worry about that, they had each other, he didn't need a dad. The way she said this always made it clear that as far as she was concerned the matter was closed.

The light was beginning to fade now, and he called Trixie, saying it was time to go. When they arrived back at the house, his mother was in the kitchen preparing sandwiches for supper. She still seemed distracted though, and they ate their food more or less in silence, Archie still feeling that his mother had somehow lost interest in him. He had begun to realise that she had a life of her own which didn't always include him, and he really had no idea how to deal with the feelings this was engendering in him.

Without realising why, his thoughts, for the first time in ages, turned to Ben and the man on the boat. He decided that he would take a ride along the towpath the following day. Now that he had Trixie, maybe the man wouldn't feel that he was trying to take Ben away from him. In any case it would be good for Trixie to have some company. Of course, he wouldn't mention it to his mother, not yet, at any rate.

Chapter Seven

When half term arrived, Alex was glad to put stressful thoughts of the past few weeks out of her mind. Her parents were thrilled to be having their grandchildren around for a few days. The weather promised to be hot and sunny even though it was still early summer. Alex was their only child and Johnny and Aby their only grandchildren, so they had a lot invested in them.

As they pulled up outside the familiar semi on the outskirts of Tidmouth, Alex felt the usual warm glow at the sight of the house she had grown up in, filled as it was, with happy memories. As an only child she had wanted for nothing. Her father, now retired, had been a history teacher at the local secondary school and her mother also worked there as school secretary for many years. So, school holidays were always special family times, and the long summer break was usually spent travelling.

Now as she waited for the door to open, she felt excited. However, when she saw her father standing there, she could see that he had lost weight and was looking older, which worried her slightly. Only to be expected, she thought to herself. They're not getting any younger; her father, Ted, was eighty next birthday and Dorothy, her mother, just a year younger. She was even more shocked when she saw her mum standing behind him. She definitely didn't look good. She was pale with dark shadows under her eyes, and she also had lost weight.

Without comment, Alex stepped forward and took her in her arms.

'Mum! How lovely to see you!' she said. 'It's been too long, hasn't it?'

'Well, we know how busy you are love,' she replied, hugging her daughter fiercely, then turning her attention to her grandchildren.

'Come here, you two, and give your old grandma a kiss! I can't believe how you've grown.'

Johnny and Aby, having embraced their grandad, stepped forward to kiss her on the cheek. Aby couldn't help measuring up against her grandma, as she always did, to see how much she'd grown since their last visit.

'Yes, taller than me now, aren't you? My goodness, you've both grown so much! It's so good to see you all,' she went on.

Dave had taken their suitcase out of the boot and now stepped into the hall, shaking hands with Ted saying,

'It's great to see you Ted, how have you been?'

'Oh, you know,' he replied, 'we keep plodding on.'

Glancing at the two of them, Dave also felt a

little uneasy. Neither of them looked too well. He was pleased they had come. They needed to find out how they really were and whether they needed help with anything.

As the week progressed Alex became more and more concerned about her mother. It was obvious she was struggling, and it wasn't just that she was getting older. She wasn't eating properly and although determined not to miss a minute of time with the children, she was obviously finding it hard to keep up with them. Alex had tried several times to find out what was wrong, but she just dismissed her concerns. She told Dave she wasn't leaving without finding out what the problem was. On the Thursday, she decided to ask her father. He was almost as dismissive as Dorothy had been but when Alex insisted that she knew something was wrong and she needed to know, he finally told her to ask her mother again. With that, Dave suggested they would all take a trip along the coast to Lyme Regis and Dave and Ted would take the children fossil hunting while Alex could spend a couple of hours alone with Dorothy, when she might be able to find out what the problem was.

The next day they piled into the car and set off for the Jurassic Coast. Johnny and Aby were excited. Fossil hunting was one of their favourite things, and they were looking forward to spending time with their dad and grandad. Alex suggested that she and Dorothy would go for a cup of tea and then perhaps take a walk along the seafront.

They found a quiet café just off the promenade and settled down to have their tea and scones. Alex lost no time in asking her mum what was wrong. At first Dorothy seemed reluctant to admit that there were any problems, but Alex insisted that she could see things weren't right and asked her outright whether she was ill. Dorothy's eyes misted up as she said,

'I knew there would be no fooling you, love. It's the big C, I'm afraid.'

'Oh mum, no! How long have you known?'

'I got the diagnosis, bowel cancer, three weeks ago. They've done a lot of tests, but I'm afraid it doesn't sound great. They are hoping they may be able to operate but they are frank, until they open me up to see how far it's spread, they won't really know whether they will be able to get rid of it completely.'

Alex's stomach churned. She was utterly shocked, just unable to grasp what all this meant.

'Well, they have made amazing strides in cancer treatment these days,' she said lamely.

'Well, it may have spread too far. I know I should have had it investigated months ago, but I just kept hoping it would go away. It will probably mean chemo of course, even after the surgery, which I'm not looking forward to. The good thing is, I'm not in any pain, not yet at any rate. That may change, but the doctor told me that they can deal successfully with that when the time comes.'

'Well that's good Mum. I just can't believe it though.

This shouldn't be happening to you, you've always kept yourself so fit. God Mum, it's just too awful.'

'It's your Dad I worry about. How he'll manage without me I have no idea.'

'Well you mustn't worry about Dad, we'll make sure he's alright, as far as we can.'

'I know you will love, but there are so many things he relies on me for. I've always been the one to deal with the banks and the internet accounts and so on. I suppose I'll just have to make sure everything's written down for him.'

'Have they given you any idea when they will do the operation?'

'Not yet love, but I imagine it will be as soon as possible. Whatever happens it's not going to be pleasant. if I agree to have the operation, depending what they find, it may involve taking part of my bowel away.'

'Oh, Mum,' Alex said, tears now trickling down her cheeks, 'but you said 'if'. Surely you will have the operation?'

'I haven't decided yet. It might be best just to accept the inevitable. Palliative care is very good these days. I could struggle on for a couple of years but honestly, is that what I really want? Operations, a colostomy bag, chemo, maybe radiation as well, and virtually no quality of life.'

Alex couldn't speak, her throat constricted with emotion, and the tears flowed freely.

'Now, you mustn't cry love. I've had a good life and

longer than most. We've all just got to come to terms with it, and you'll have to help the children to deal with it all when the time comes.'

At the mention of the children, Alex's heart jumped in her chest. They will be devastated to lose the grandma they love so dearly, who's always been there, giving them nothing but love all their lives.

Other people in the café had by now noticed how upset Alex was and Dorothy took hold of both of her hands across the table. They just sat quietly like that until Alex had regained her composure, then Dorothy said,

'Come on love, let's get out of here and take a walk.'

When they left the café they strolled arm in arm along the seafront, neither of them speaking, both deep in their own thoughts, but valuing these precious moments they were spending together. After an hour or so they made their way to the Harbour Inn where they were to meet Dave and Ted and the children. Alex saw them in the distance, striding along without a care in the world, while she stood there holding onto her mother's arm as she realised her own world had changed forever, as theirs soon would.

Later that night when she and Dave were in bed, Alex couldn't stop the tears as she gave him the news. He was shocked, of course. He was very fond of both Dorothy and Ted. They had always treated him as a son, not just a son -in-law. He had never considered that one day they may not be there anymore. It was a lot to take in. Being of a pragmatic turn of mind, his thoughts turned to how all this would be managed. They would need to make sure that Ted and Dorothy had enough support as things progressed. Would she want to go into a hospice? They would need to be making enquiries. All this was going through his mind as he comforted his wife, and it was a couple of hours before they finally fell into an exhausted sleep.

The next day they were due to leave. Alex wanted to stay with her parents, but they insisted that she must go, she had her work to do and they were fine, they had everything they needed for now, they reassured her. Dorothy promised to tell Alex if there was anything else they needed in the future. As they hadn't told the children, they couldn't go into anything else at that point, but Alex promised to ring them soon. As Alex hugged Ted, she just said quietly,

'I'm so sorry dad. I'll ring later to see if there's anything we can do.'

Her father just gave her a fierce hug, hanging on as if he never wanted to let go. Alex gave her mother a special embrace before climbing into the car and then they were off, leaving her parents standing by the gate. As the car turned the corner, Alex turned to look in their direction and blew them a kiss before they disappeared from view.

Chapter Eight

A few days after the trip to the Safari Park, Alice decided to ring Sam to see if she fancied coming over for a barbecue the next day. She couldn't help feeling that they had some unfinished business. Sam had left so abruptly. They had had a lovely day which she seemed to enjoy and it was odd that she wouldn't come in to share their supper. The next day Alice told Archie that Sam was coming over for a barbecue later on, if the weather held.

As if she hadn't seen enough of her already this week he thought to himself.

'I think I'll go for a ride this morning mum,' he told her in an innocent voice, knowing full well that he would be riding along the canal to see if Ben was back.

'Okay love,' his mother replied rather absently, as she was clearing away the breakfast things.

Taking his bike out of the shed he tied Trixie's lead to the handlebars, waved goodbye to Alice through the kitchen window and set off along the alleyway towards the road. He deliberately didn't take the direct route to the canal, as he didn't want Alice guessing where he was going. He knew she still wasn't keen on him cycling along the towpath. He was excited by his own boldness in deliberately, indirectly defying his mother but justified it by reminding himself that now she had her friend Sam, she wasn't really interested in what he was doing anyway.

In five minutes, he was riding happily along the tow-path away from the town. His excitement disappeared however, as Ben and the man were still nowhere to be seen. After a couple of miles or so he reluctantly turned his bike around and set off back towards home. Somehow, he felt let down. It was some time since he'd last seen them, and he had expected that by now they would have returned. He passed the spot where he had first met Ben and felt sad that Trixie wouldn't be meeting him today. However, he knew that people didn't travel far on the canal and that eventually they would probably return. If he came by often, he would be bound to find them there one day.

When he arrived back home, as he approached the house, he could see Sam's car already on the drive-way. He didn't know whether to be pleased or not. He did enjoy a barbecue but the thought of his mother constantly looking at Sam in that peculiar way gave him that funny, nameless feeling once again. He rode round to the back gate, propping his bike up against the shed and untying Trixie. His mum wasn't in the kitchen, so he went through to the lounge.

He was shocked to find her in Sam's arms, and, horror of horrors, they were actually kissing! He didn't know what to do, he was acutely embarrassed at finding them like that. He was confused. He was angry that this woman was actually kissing his mother in a way that a man would. He did know that some women prefer other women, but he had never suspected that was how his mum felt. What did this mean for him? Where did he fit into this situation?

Sam and Alice sprang apart as Archie turned on his heels and ran up the stairs to his room. Alice followed, arriving as the door slammed in her face. She knocked gently saying

'Archie, please can I come in?'

There was a muffled reply and Alice slowly opened the door. Archie had thrown himself face down on his bed and didn't look up as she entered. He couldn't. He was too embarrassed. How could his mother do this? The kiss he'd seen wasn't a friend-to-friend light peck on the cheek. This was something else. They had been standing with their bodies pressed close and he'd seen enough on the tele to know that this sort of kiss didn't stop there.

'Archie,' his mother said gently, kneeling down beside the bed, 'I'm sorry you had to find out like that, but Sam and I are really good friends now, and that's how really good friends show that they care about each other.'

'I know that!' Archie exclaimed into his pillow, 'but why do you need her anyway? It's always been just us but now she's around you've changed! You don't listen to me anymore!'

'Sweetheart,' Alice replied softly, touching his shoulder.

He shrugged off her hand, declaring 'Go away!'

By now Sam had appeared at the doorway and said quietly,

'Leave the lad Alice, let him think it through.'

Reluctantly, Alice got up and slowly walked towards the door saying,

'Please come down when you're ready Archie,' to which he replied with a grunt, burying his head further into his pillow. With that, she and Sam made their way downstairs.

Trixie had followed Archie upstairs and now lay down beside the bed, sensing that he was upset. They stayed like that for the next hour or so, Archie trying to understand what had just happened. He was a bright lad and understood that life had just changed, however much he wished it hadn't. It wasn't turning out to be a good day, he thought to himself. He'd already been disappointed not to find Ben on the canal, and now this! Life sucks, he thought. Then another thought struck him. Maybe this thing with Sam won't last anyway. When his mother sees how much it upsets him, perhaps it will put her off her and she'll choose to go back the way they were before. Well, he certainly wouldn't be making her choice any easier, she could be sure of that, he thought angrily.

Spurred on by this embryo of a plan forming in his head, he finally got up and went downstairs, Trixie trotting obediently behind him. He found his mother in the kitchen, preparing food for the barbecue and Sam was in the garden mowing the lawn. Even this annoyed Archie. How dare she mow our lawn, he thought, rather illogically.

'Hello love,' his mother said with rather enforced brightness.

Archie just grunted, determined not to make this easy for her.

'Do you want to help me with the food?' she asked him.

He mumbled something about play-station, and shambled off into the living room, leaving Alice feeling upset and wondering if he would ever accept the fact that she had a life of her own. The feelings Sam had awakened in her had taken her completely by surprise, and she was powerless to resist them. She wanted her, needed her love more than she could ever have thought possible. She had never been in love like this before. Of course, this situation brought other difficulties which would have to be faced eventually. If she wanted to be close to Sam, she knew that at some point she would have to know about Archie, which terrified her. At that point she deliberately cut off this train of thought and went out into the garden to see how she was getting on with mowing the lawn.

As Trixie followed her out, Sam said,

'I guess Archie's come down then. How does he seem?'

'Pretty unresponsive. He's gone off to play on the

play-station. I just hope he can come to terms with things.'

'Well, it can't be easy for him, seeing us like that, and apart from that, until now he's had you all to himself. I'm guessing his dad has never really been around?' she enquired.

'No, he hasn't,' Alice replied with emphasis, and rather too quickly, indicating to Sam that it wasn't a subject for discussion, and then immediately turned the conversation in a more comfortable direction. 'The lawn's not looking too bad, is it?'

Sam smiled knowingly to herself then agreed,

'It's not bad but could do with raking, there's quite a bit of moss here and there.'

The rest of the day passed by without incident. Archie continued to be sullen and unresponsive, but Alice and Sam just ignored his surliness, feeling he was best left alone to come to terms with the situation in his own time.

During the next few weeks Sam was around most of the time and in spite of himself Archie began to feel more comfortable about it. It turned out that she liked play-station, and they had several sessions which Archie largely won. On Fridays they all went shopping together and he had to admit that it felt good. Sam was generous and sometimes even bought him a new play-station game. There had been no repeat of the kissing incident, so Archie wasn't sure where all this was going.

Chapter Nine

Alex had kept in close contact with her Mum and Dad. After spending some time resisting, Dorothy had finally been persuaded by Ted and Alex to have the surgery. The date of the operation was set and Alex managed to get a few days off work to visit them to help to sort things out in readiness, and to support her father. She had been shocked at the deterioration in her Mum in the few short weeks since she'd last seen her.

Operation day dawned and Alex drove them both to the hospital. Ted had been in a highly agitated state, obviously afraid he might lose his partner of fifty years. When they checked in to reception they were directed up to the Surgical Ward and ushered into a side ward where the pre-operation checks were carried out. Once Dorothy had settled in, the anaesthetist arrived. It seemed the purpose of his visit was largely to reassure the patient, and he carefully explained everything that would be happening.

Dorothy was sitting in up in the bed, leaning

wearily against the white cotton pillowcase and Alex was shocked at how pale and frail she looked. Not for the first time, she wondered whether she and Ted had been right to persuade her to have the operation. The anaesthetist was holding the consent form, pointing out that no surgery was one hundred percent safe, always carrying a certain level of risk. However, if she was content to go ahead, he said, would she be kind enough to sign the form. After a few moments' hesitation, when she glanced first at Ted and then Alex, Dorothy took the pen from the doctor and quickly signed her name. So that was it. No turning back now.

Within half an hour she was being wheeled out of the room and down the corridor to the operating theatre. The anaesthetist had told Alex and Ted the operation may take quite a while, depending what they found, but it would be at least an hour before they had finished. Once Dorothy had been taken to theatre, Ted and Alex went down to the restaurant for a coffee while they waited for news. The nursing staff had promised to ring Alex when her mother was out of surgery.

They stayed in the restaurant for around ninety minutes until they could stand it no longer, then made their way back up to the ward. Dorothy was still in surgery, which they took to be a good sign. Maybe they had been able to do something other than just looking, after all. The nurse on duty told them that once the operation was over, more than likely she would be taken to the intensive care unit for a little while to ensure that she was stable before being transferred back onto the surgical ward.

Another hour dragged by while they waited in the relative's room. Finally, the surgeon came to tell them that the operation had been largely successful. They had removed the cancer but unfortunately it had meant removing part of Dorothy's bowel, so that she would need to have a colostomy bag. Ted and Alex were obviously relieved that Dorothy had come through the operation, but a little shocked she'd been given a bag, the one thing she had dreaded most. He told them she would also need chemo, to destroy any remaining cancerous cells. He said he thought they had removed it completely as far as he could tell, but it wasn't a precise science, and it was better to be safe than sorry. They asked when they could see her, and the surgeon said that she was in intensive care but as she was now conscious they could visit her briefly.

They followed him up to the IC unit and were both shocked to see her lying there with tubes everywhere, with her eyes closed, looking helpless and vulnerable. Ted was visibly moved. He had been terrified for the last few months that he was about to lose the woman he'd shared his life with for over half a century. Seeing her lying there brought it home to him just how imminent that eventuality had been. He knew that she wasn't out of the woods yet, but after what the surgeon had said, although she would need care, he felt he would keep her with him for a while yet. Tears of relief trickled down his face.

Alex put her arm around his shoulders to comfort him, then said quietly,

'Hello Mum.'

Dorothy opened her eyes and they were relieved to see that wonderful smile of hers, then seeing her husband with tears in his eyes, she said, rather drowsily,

'Don't be upset love, I'm going to be fine now, you'll see.'

Alex thought how typical that was of her, to be thinking not about herself but about her husband, wanting to reassure him above anything else.

'Mum, I'm so glad that's over. You had us worried there for a while. It seemed to take so long!'

Dorothy was drifting off to sleep again, so they decided to leave her to get some rest.

Alex stayed with her dad for a couple more days until Dorothy was stable enough to be moved back to the surgical ward, then after visiting her once more and reassuring them both that she would be back if they needed her, she left them at the hospital and set off for home.

Driving back she reflected on the past few days. She was relieved of course that her Mum had come through the operation, but she knew this was unlikely to be the end of the matter. On the contrary, it was probably just the beginning of a long hard road ahead for her mother. There was the management of the colostomy bag which in itself, and at her age, would probably be life-limiting. Then there was the chemo to get through. Alex had had a friend who had died from breast cancer, and she knew only too well, the toll that pumping a body full of poisons could take, and at her mum's age, she was afraid that she wouldn't be able to stand it.

The house was empty when she arrived home, the children still at school and Dave presumably at the office. He sometimes worked from home and she was disappointed he wasn't there. She badly needed a hug. It had been an emotional few days and now that she was back in familiar surroundings she let go of the brave face she'd been putting on and relaxed a little, allowing herself the luxury of shedding a tear or two. Poor Mum and Dad, she thought, they've got so much ahead of them, and I wish I was nearer to them and able to give them more help. She went upstairs and had a shower then dried her hair and dressed, then rang Dave to find out what time he'd be home.

'Hi love,' he said, 'when did you get back?'

'About an hour ago,' Alex replied.

'How were things in Tidmouth?'

'Oh, you know, it's early days, Mum is in good spirits but you know her, she's more worried about Dad than herself. I'll fill you in with the details later. What time do you think you'll be home?'

'Now I know you're back, I'll leave straight away, I can bring this stuff with me, so I'll see you in about half an hour.'

'That's great love, I could really do with a cuddle right now!'

***

Over the next few months Alex visited Tidmouth as often as she could. She was utterly torn between her work, Dave and the children, and her parents. She often felt she was being pulled apart, trying to do her best to be wherever she was needed most, but her best never seemed good enough.

Work was especially demanding, with several harrowing cases to deal with, one of them involving child abuse and another where the cruelty meted out eventually led to the child's death. Alex felt she would never understand what led some people to attack a child. Of course, it wasn't her job to understand why they did it, it was up to her to bring the perpetrator before the courts, and trust that they would at least deliver justice for the victim. When there was a successful outcome, she felt that all the hard work had been worthwhile, she had done her job and it felt like the best job in the world. However, when the conviction failed, it was difficult to take. She tried not to see it as a personal failure, but it was hard not to, particularly seeing the devastated reaction of the victim's relatives.

Dorothy was soldiering on with the chemo, needing fortnightly treatments which involved a fifty-minute drive each way to the nearest oncology centre. Alex worried about Ted having to drive so far. He didn't seem as confident behind the wheel as he used to, but

Dorothy wasn't up to it, so there was no alternative. She was always relieved to hear that they had arrived back home safely.

Dorothy's hair began to fall out, leaving noticeable bald patches and she had been given a wig to wear. Each chemo treatment left her feeling exhausted, but eventually it was over. When she next had a routine check-up, all seemed well. She had learned to cope well with the colostomy bag, and it didn't seem to inhibit her too much. She and Ted started to go out again for the odd meal, or the cinema and Alex relaxed a little while of course, still keeping in close contact with them.

Chapter Ten

The winter wore on, and Christmas came and went. Archie had to admit that it was good having Sam around. She was funny and kind, and as well as that, his Mum seemed happy all the time these days.

However, all that changed one Saturday morning in early March. He woke early and decided he'd like to take a ride along the towpath again. Maybe Ben would be back by now. He jumped out of bed and went to ask Alice if he could go. As he opened her bedroom door, he was shocked to the core to find that she wasn't alone. Sam was there, in her bed! She was asleep on his mum's shoulder, her other arm thrown across her in an intimate embrace. In his astonishment he stood stock still until Sam opened her eyes and saw him standing there. Archie turned on his heels and ran down the stairs.

Once again, Alice tried to explain to Archie that she was really fond of Sam, that she made her happy, and that in fact, it was likely that she would soon be moving in with them permanently. Archie made no comment, but he was thinking plenty. Of course, he knew that some women preferred other women, and even though he had seen them kissing once, months ago, he had begun to think he'd read too much into that as there had been no repetition of it. After all, she must have preferred a man once, or how was he born? Well, that was it then, if they were a couple, he would never again have his mother's complete attention. He also realised he would never have a Dad either. *She* would always be there. There was nothing he could do about it. He would just have to get on with his own life from now on.

It was a week later that Sam moved in. As the weeks passed, Sam and Alice became more and more wrapped up in each other. No decision was made now without the two of them discussing it. Where once Alice might have chatted to Archie about things, it was to Sam she turned for a second opinion, and he was just informed as to what was going to happen. He began to feel isolated, as though his feelings and thoughts didn't matter anymore. He felt he was shrinking.

It was in this frame of mind that he took his bike and Trixie one Saturday morning and headed for the towpath. As he rounded the bend, he saw Ben in the distance. In fact, Trixie saw him first and started barking. As they drew nearer Ben started barking also and straining at his lead which had been tied to the gangplank of the boat. The man was sitting by the rudder reading, and looked up to see Archie riding towards them, with a golden lab in tow.

In spite of himself, Jack felt a surge of excitement at seeing the lad again. He felt he needed to know more about this boy who had awakened in him feelings he thought he'd never have again. Archie stopped and jumped off his bike and started to ruffle Ben's fur. The dog obviously remembered the lad. Trixie was excited too and immediately curious about this creature who her master was making such a fuss of. Jack stood up,

'I wondered whether we would see you here,' he said, in a not unfriendly tone.

Archie smiled and replied, 'I've been looking for you a lot. Mum lets me ride along here on my own now I've got Trixie.'

'She's a great looking dog, have you had her long?'

'About eight months, since just after I saw you and Ben here last. I was sad you'd gone, and I thought I wouldn't see Ben again so mum got me Trixie so I wouldn't be sad anymore.'

'That's good of your mum, and Trixie looks like she's a great friend for you. Look,' Jack went on, 'I'm just about to make a bit of a snack, would you like something? A bacon sandwich perhaps?'

Archie hesitated, unsure what his mum would think. Then he decided she was too wrapped up in Sam to even care, so he said,

'Thanks, I love bacon sarnies.'

With that they tied the two dogs up together, giving them a bowl of water and a couple of biscuits each, then Archie clambered aboard the Lady Louise for the first time. He'd never actually been on a narrowboat before, and it felt like he was entering another world. Everything seemed to be made of wood, apart from the metal sink. There was a bed, a small sofa and a table with a bench seat. The ceiling seemed very low but high enough for the man to stand. In the corner was something that looked like some kind of fire.

'This is great,' Archie observed, then tentatively asked, 'what's your name?'

'I'm Jack Long' he said. Archie nodded and reminded him of his name.

'Well, it's Archibald really, but nobody calls me that, because I don't like it. I don't know why mum called me that.'

'Maybe it was your dad's name, or a grandad's?' Jack ventured.

'I don't know what my dad's name was, I never knew him,' Archie replied.

Something stirred in Jack's mind, but he pushed it aside as being fanciful nonsense.

They took their bacon sandwiches up onto the roof, to sit in the sunshine to eat them, and drink the cans of Coke Jack had produced from the cupboard over the sink. Archie was pleased with the Coke. He was never allowed it at home. 'It rots your teeth,' his mum usually said whenever he asked for one. Still, he thought, one can't do much harm, and drank it eagerly.

After they'd eaten, they sat for an hour or so, chatting easily. Jack asked him about school. What subject did he like best? Did he have lots of friends? What were they called? Then Archie asked Jack whether he liked living on a boat.

'I certainly do,' Jack replied. 'I enjoy being out in nature, and I like my own company, except for Ben of course.'

They glanced down at the dogs and they seemed perfectly happy lying side by side on the grass. The sun was shining on the water gently lapping around the boat, and they settled into a companiable silence for a while, until Jack suddenly said,

'Perhaps you ought to be getting back home now, your mum will wonder where you've got to.'

'No, she won't,' Archie replied, 'she doesn't bother about me now. She's got a live-in girlfriend.'

'Oh, I see. Well, I'm sure she still 'does bother about you' as you say, so you'd better be off now.'

'Ok, I suppose,' Archie grudgingly agreed. He felt happy here. He felt valued and didn't really want to leave, but he eventually got up and jumped down onto the gangplank, saying

'Come on Trixie, time to go.'

At that Trixie's ears pricked up and she dragged herself to her feet as Archie stood his bike up and tied her lead to the handlebars.

'Bye then Jack,' he said. 'Will you be staying here for a while?'

'Probably,' Jack confirmed, 'drop by again if you like.'

Archie grinned and said he would, in fact, probably

tomorrow, then gave Jack a wave as he rode off along the towpath.

***

After that, Archie began to spend more and more time with Jack. Sometimes they would take long walks along the towpath, or through the woods, collecting berries, edible mushrooms, or wild garlic, or even simply sitting on top of the boat painting. At other times they would play card games, or Jack would teach him how to play chess. Of course, Archie still felt unable to tell Alice about his growing friendship with Jack and she rarely asked where he'd been when he went out on his bike. He had to be careful not to give the secret away by letting her know he could play chess or card games they had never played at home. He did feel a bit guilty about not being absolutely straight with her, but he didn't want to risk being prevented from seeing Jack and Ben, and so he kept it to himself.

As for Jack, he thoroughly enjoyed having the boy around. He felt a real empathy towards him. He was about the age that Toby would have been by now, he thought to himself one day. For one brief moment he allowed himself to indulge in the thought, then told himself not to be stupid, Toby was gone and that was that. Until, one day they decided to have a swim in the canal and Archie had taken off his t shirt. As he turned to jump in the water, Jack's legs nearly gave way as he saw the strawberry shaped birth mark on the lad's back. It was right between his shoulder blades in exactly the same place Toby's had been, but larger.

His mind was spinning now. Archie had said he hadn't known his dad, hadn't he? What if ... Surely it was too much of a coincidence? He realised he couldn't say anything to the lad without some kind of proof and he was a long way off having that.

Of course, once that thought was in his mind, he couldn't shake it off. Every time he saw Archie after that he had an enormous urge to tell him. Then he thought how huge that would be. The boy had been brought up by his 'mum' and hadn't known anything different, and he may easily be wrong about this anyway. Lots of people have birthmarks. It must surely just be a coincidence. So this is how he tried to rationalise it, but it just wouldn't go away.

Things got so intense that he felt he needed to take a break to try to sort out his feelings and what, if anything, he ought to do about it. He did need some work doing on the boat anyway and decided to sail it up to the boatyard a couple of miles further along the canal for a few days. The following Saturday when Archie turned up he told him he would be away for a week or so, and he would see him on his return. Archie was disappointed but said he would come back the following weekend.

Chapter Eleven

It was Sunday and Alice was luxuriating in a hot bath, contemplating life in general and her own more specifically. She was falling more deeply in love with Sam every day. She was everything she had ever needed. She was a kind and generous lover, and the sex was exquisite. Archie now seemed to accept her too, and that made her happy. In fact, life was good, very good, apart from one nagging doubt.

What to do about Archie?

As she lay there, for once she allowed herself to remember. The first time she laid eyes on him, she knew he was hers. She deserved him. After what she'd been through, he had to be hers. She had been so certain, and then, there he was in his pushchair, right in front of her. It was so easy. She took hold of the handles and walked, didn't even run. Round the corner, round another corner, and away. She had been amazed no one in the flats where she lived ever questioned where he had come from. Of course, she hadn't lived there very long, just a couple of months, after walking out of her parents' home and catching the train with no real idea where she was going or how she was going to live. She had never forgiven them for taking her baby away and as soon as she was able, had plotted to leave them and never go back and that's what she'd done. Now she had her baby back and her life could really begin.

She had found work at a nursery which meant she could take Archie with her and when he started school she managed to train as a teaching assistant, and after topping up her qualifications at college, a teacher. She'd done well and was proud of herself. She had worked hard and made a good home for him, but now, she told herself, was her time. Of course, she knew that if she was to share her life with Sam, which she longed to do, one day she would have to explain about Archie. Surely, she would understand though? If she loved her as much as she said she did, she would know that she had had no choice, and she only had to look at Archie, how happy and healthy he was, to know it had been the right thing to do. Yes, she would understand.

She became aware that the water had become quite chilled and climbed out of the bath, quickly drying herself and putting on her dressing gown. Sam had said she would take her out for a meal tonight, some-where special, as she had something she wanted to ask her. She was excited. Could she mean what she thought she meant? It was too early to get ready for the evening, so she pulled on her jeans and sweat-shirt and trotted downstairs to make herself a cup of tea. Sam had gone out to do a bit of shopping. Archie was on the PlayStation. She had just settled down with her cup of tea when he came into the kitchen in search of food, looking a bit fed up.

'Something wrong?' she asked.

Suddenly, Archie had had enough of telling her half-truths. He had an uncontrollable urge to unburden himself. What would she care anyway, he thought, if he had made friends with Jack and Ben? He was old enough now to make up his own mind, he told himself. After taking a deep breath he said,

'I'm fed up because Jack and Ben will be away for a whole week.'

Silence ensued.

'What did you just say?!' Alice exclaimed.

He repeated it.

'What the hell do you mean? Jack and Ben will be away! Have you been seeing them again?'

'Yes I have,' he asserted. 'Why, what does it matter? You don't care who I see!'

At that moment Sam walked in.

'Don't speak to your mother like that,' she shouted.

'And don't you speak to me like that, you have no right!!' Archie shouted back.

'He's just said he's been seeing that chap on the boat again, when he knows he shouldn't be!'

'Why shouldn't I?!' Archie shouted. 'He likes me. He talks to me and listens to what I have to say, which is more than you do!'

'Well you won't be seeing him again, I can tell you that,' Sam said with some conviction.

'You can't stop me,' he asserted and with that he ran out of the room, jumped on his bike that he'd left propped against the shed and rode off, leaving his mother calling after him,

'Archie! Come back here, right now!'

'Let him go love,' said Sam, 'he'll be back when he's hungry. He's not even taken Trixie with him.'

Archie rode like the wind to the canal and along the towpath. Discovering that Jack had already left, he decided to carry on to the boatyard. He knew it was a fair way along but there was no way he was going home. He wanted to be with Jack. Half an hour or so later he arrived at the boatyard, and found the Lady Louise tied up alongside. The light was beginning to fade now and Jack was lighting the lantern he kept on the back of the boat. He saw Archie riding along the towpath and called out to him.

'Archie! What are you doing here? You should be at home, it's nearly dark!'

'I've left!' Archie declared.

'What do you mean, left?'

'I mean I'm coming to stay with you. I don't want to live with them anymore, they don't want me anyway!'

'You'd better tell me what's happened,' Jack said.

Archie told him about the argument and what it was about. Jack was shocked that Archie hadn't told his mum that he'd been seeing him and said as much.

'Well, Archie, you can't stay here. I can't look after you, and your mother will be out of her mind with worry. It's too dark now to ride home or to sail the boat back. We'll have to give her a ring so she can come and get you.'

'No!' Archie shouted. 'I won't go back! They don't want me!'

'I'm sure you're wrong there, lad,' Jack assured him. 'Now, give me her number and I'll call her. Right now please, Archie,' he added firmly.

Reluctantly, Archie told him Alice's number and he quickly called it.

'Hello,' she answered, 'who is this?'

'You don't know me, my name is Jack, and I'm ringing to tell you that your son Archie is here, with me.'

'You're the boatman! What are you doing with my son!' Alice shouted.

'Look, he just turned up here ten minutes ago and I'm ringing to tell you so you can come and pick him up. It's too dark now for him to ride back along the towpath.'

He told her where he was and gave her the postcode of the boatyard.

'He had no right to come to you! He knows that! I'll kill him when I get my hands on him! We'll be there in ten minutes,' Alice asserted.

It was dark as Alice and Sam arrived at the Marina. Jack was waiting with Archie at the gate as they got out of the car and strode across the carpark.

'Archie!' Alice exclaimed, 'What do you think you're playing at! Get in the car, this minute.'

Sam joined in, saying,

'Come on Archie, let's put your bike in the boot,' and started wheeling the bike towards the car.

'I don't want to come home!' Archie shouted. 'You can't make me! I want to stay here with Jack.'

At this point, Jack stepped forward into the sphere of the security light, saying gently,

'Look, Archie, I've told you, you can't stay with me on the boat. You need to go home with your mum.'

Archie looked crestfallen, but realising he had no choice, shambled off after Sam and got in the car.

For the first time, Alice looked directly at Jack and it was as if a bolt of lightning struck her. The hairs on the back of her neck stood up. The likeness was unmistakeable. The shape of his head, the way one eye was slightly larger than the other, the curls. The sight of him took her right back to that beach the first time she'd seen him. The clincher was her memory, just rekindled, of reading the newspaper article about a toddler going missing, and the television appeal showing this man and a woman, presumably his wife, appealing for information. She remembered feeling sorry for them, but of course it had been nothing to do with her!

Jack saw the fleeting expression of recognition that had flashed across the woman's face. Could this be the face he'd scrutinised inside his head for years, wondering who she was, and whether she was the one who'd taken Toby? Was Archie his little Toby? He thought about the way he had immediately felt a connection to the lad; the way his presence had melted the protective wall he had so carefully constructed around himself, and suddenly he was certain. It was Toby!

All these thoughts were spinning round their brains as they stood in silence, just looking into each other's eyes. This was too big a thing for either of them to say anything at that moment. Jack briefly considered confronting her there and then but before he could say anything, she turned on her heels and almost ran to the car, jumping in the front seat and slamming the door. In another minute they were gone, leaving Jack standing at the gate, wondering what on earth he should do next.

As he walked back to the boat, another desperate thought occurred to him. He was certain she had recognised him so what would she do next? Would she stay and fight him and try to prove that Archie was hers, or would she run, taking Archie with her, stealing his Toby once again! He could do nothing tonight, but decided that tomorrow he must act before it was too late.

**

Alice sat silently in the front seat of the car. Her mind was in turmoil. She was certain the man was the man from the beach. Her world was about to come tumbling down. She would have to act, but to do what? Could she fight, convince the authorities that Archie was hers which in her mind of course he was. But could she risk anyone taking her baby away again? She'd run once, she could run again. Take him away. She glanced across at Sam. Could she tell her? Risk her not understanding, would she be prepared to run with her? Her head was spinning. She was sure the man who called himself Jack had seen the panic in her face, and she had seen the light of recognition in his. What would he do now? Go to the police?

Archie sat silently in the back seat. He felt humiliated that the adults in his life never seemed to take any notice of what he wanted, and he felt powerless to make them. When they arrived home, he immediately ran up to his room and threw himself down on his bed, no longer able to hold back the tears.

Alice had still said nothing to Sam. She needed space to think this through.

Sam made an attempt at conversation, saying,

'Try not to be too hard on the lad Alice. He's obviously unhappy. We must try talking to him tomorrow and hopefully be able to get to the bottom of what's bothering him.'

The last thing Alice wanted was for anyone to 'get to the bottom' of things. She now understood why her son had been so attracted to this man. She was angry with herself that she hadn't spotted it before things got so serious. If she had met him the first time she'd ridden along the towpath with Archie to find him, she would have understood and maybe could have put a stop to it before they developed a relationship deep enough for Archie to go secretly, behind her back, to spend time with him. Now it was too late. She knew neither the man nor her son would give up easily on this relationship, especially now.

Chapter Twelve

As she lay in bed that night beside Sam, a plan began to form in her head. She now knew that however much it hurt her to leave Sam behind, if she wanted to keep her son, she must do exactly that. In the early years she had formulated and prepared a plan for just such an eventuality. Over time, she had become convinced it would never be needed, but now fate had taken a hand. The very thing she had always dreaded had come to pass. She now had to implement the plan. She had saved some money in a savings account she never used for anything else. She also had some cash stashed away for emergencies. She would take Archie, telling him they were going on an adventure, and head north. She had sussed out the cottage in the far west of Scotland years ago. If it was free, she would take him there until she could think what to do next. As a child she had spent many happy holidays in the Scottish Highlands. She knew the cottage she'd selected was pretty remote and she thought they would be safe there for a few weeks at least.

***

The next day she told Sam she felt unwell, and after a sleepless night, she looked it. She asked her to give her apologies at work, and kissed her as she left, knowing that it may be the last time, which broke her heart, but she knew she had no alternative other than to leave. Sam always went into school early to prepare for the day, leaving before Archie. Once she had gone, she woke her son up and told him she'd decided they would go away for a few days, saying that after what had happened, she felt it would be good to spend some time alone with him. Just the two of them, and Trixie, of course.

Archie didn't understand and said they would be expecting him at school. She told him she had rung the headmaster and explained to him that they would be away for a few days. She said that after she had explained how important she felt it was right now, he had agreed to allow him to take a little time off. Of course, she had done no such thing, but Archie was convinced.

He was now warming to the idea. Time alone with his mum and his dog! Things would be just like they were before Sam arrived. He asked where they were going, and Alice said she wasn't sure yet but that he should go and pack a few things to take with him. In the meantime, taking the car out of the garage she loaded it up with essentials, throwing in the pop-up tent and camping gear, just in case. She loaded a couple of carrier bags of food from the cupboards and packed the cool bag with items from the freezer.

She felt they would have enough food for a couple of weeks at least.

Checking the cottage on the Airbnb site, she was delighted to see that the next three weeks were free. She booked them, saving the postcode on her phone. When she checked the route on the internet, she could see it was over five hundred miles away, meaning more than ten hours driving time. They would have to break their journey somewhere around the Scottish Borders. She went upstairs and packed her bag and toiletries then checked on Archie who by now was ready for the off.

Alice decided they should eat a decent breakfast as she would prefer not to stop too soon on their journey, wanting to put as many miles as possible between them and the man, before he had time to take any action. After they had finished, they fed Trixie then piled into the car, ready for their adventure, or so Archie thought. She locked up the house after taking one last look around. She had reluctantly decided she couldn't even risk leaving a note for Sam, telling herself maybe she'd be able to ring her once things were settled.

With half a tank of petrol in the car, she decided not to fill up locally, but would pick some up on the motorway. She didn't set the satnav on her phone, not wanting to alarm Archie by showing him how far she intended to take him. In any case, she had seen enough police dramas to know that she should turn off her phone while they travelled. Having checked the route she could see that once they were on the M4, at least until the Borders, it was motorway all the way. When they stopped for the night, she would make a note of the rest of the route. They were well up the M5 when Alice stopped at the services to fill the car up with petrol. They took a short break to pick up a couple of pasties and drinks and she also bought an AA road atlas so that she would be able to plan her route without switching her phone back on.

The motorway was busy but they made steady progress. Archie was quiet. He made a couple of attempts to find out where they were going but Alice made it pretty clear he was wasting his time. As is always the case when the destination is unknown, the journey seemed endless. This trip wasn't working out to be as enjoyable as he had thought it might be.

***

After a restless night full of strange dreams, Jack had woken with a headache, feeling as though he'd hardly slept at all. Immediately remembering the events of the previous night, he rose and dressed quickly. He knew he had to act fast. The woman had recognised him. He was convinced of that, and he realised she would have two choices; fight or flight. Given that DNA technology could soon prove that Archie was in fact Toby, he realised she would almost certainly run, taking Toby away from him once again. This would of course prove once and for all that he was indeed his son, otherwise why should she run? Without even waiting to eat breakfast, only making time to feed Ben and take him into the woods, he put him back in the boat, and set off to walk to the nearest police station, about a mile away.

When he arrived, a young woman at the desk took his name and asked him who he would like to speak to. He realised what he was about to say would seem unbelievable. Nevertheless, he launched into an explanation; that after ten years, his son who had been abducted, age two, had suddenly reappeared, and the person who had taken him in the first place was living with him in this very town. He said he had met her last night and was afraid she'd recognised him and may decide to run off with his son again.

Predictably, as she listened to him, the policewoman looked sceptical but replied patiently, saying she would find someone to speak to him and take down the details, asking him to wait. Five minutes later a young man who he assumed was a rookie detective, appeared and ushered him into a room at the side of the waiting area, notebook in hand. He introduced himself as DC Cotton, gesturing to Jack to sit down. He began by asking Jack what exactly he had come for. Impatiently, Jack said he had already told the policewoman at the desk, but then went on to repeat it, as Neil made notes in his book.

'Right,' he said when Jack paused expectantly, 'Let's get a few details down.'

He asked Jack all the usual questions. Names, addresses etc. Jack realised he didn't even have an address for the lad he believed to be his son. He'd never had occasion to ask Archie where he lived. He did know however that his 'mother' was a school-teacher at the local comprehensive and was called Alice Cookson.

'Of course,' Jack said, 'she may have changed her name since she took my son.'

'Let's not jump to conclusions, Sir,' the young detective said, in line, no doubt with his recent training. 'We will of course make some enquiries. Try not to worry, we'll do our best to get to the bottom of this.'

Jack didn't feel the constable had grasped the urgency of the situation.

'Look, it's over twelve hours since she must have realised I had recognised her. She could already have taken him and be miles away by now.'

'I understand sir, and we will let you know as soon as we get any news.'

Reluctantly Jack left the police station and headed back to the boat. He needed to let Ben out, and in any case, frustratingly, as he didn't even have an address for Archie, there was nothing more he could do for the moment.

***

Neil Cotton went upstairs to the office and knocked on Alex's door.

'Come in,' she called, 'what can I do for you Neil?'

'We've just had a chap in, called Jack Long, Boss. He said that someone stole his son ten years ago and now she's turned up with the boy. He thinks she recognised him and is concerned that she may take the boy away again.'

The name Jack Long seemed vaguely familiar to Alex, stirring a recollection of a little boy being taken from the promenade at Tidmouth, and she thought that must also be about ten years ago.

'Did Mr Long say where his son had originally been taken from, Neil?'

'He said he was taken in Tidmouth.'

Alex was now certain. She remembered the details being circulated round the county, and she also remembered her mum and dad talking about how sad it was. There had been an appeal on television by the boy's parents too.

'OK Neil, I remember the case. It was very sad. The mother in particular was broken by it and in the end I believe, she committed suicide. How did you leave it with Mr Long?'

'I said we'd look into it. He gave me the name of the woman, she's a teacher at the comp, but he doesn't have an address for her.'

'OK, can you get onto the school to confirm that and maybe get her address. Meanwhile I'll give Tidmouth a ring and get everything sent through, just in case.

***

It was half past four when Sam arrived home from work. She was surprised to find no one around. She checked upstairs to see if Alice was having a lie down and was confused to find the bedroom in some dis-array. The bed was unmade, and the wardrobe door was wide open. A couple of the drawers were partly open, as though someone had been hastily searching for something. Checking the bathroom again she was shocked to see that Alice's toothbrush and the tooth-paste was gone. Alarm bells started ringing in her head. She quickly went into Archie's room, and the situation was the same there.

Practically running down the stairs she went out to the garage. Her car was gone! Had she taken Archie away for a break somewhere? But why hadn't she said anything? She'd not even left a note! Sam didn't know what to do next. She immediately rang Archie's school to check whether he had been in school. His form teacher told her that she hadn't seen him all day and no-one had called to explain why.

Sam realised this meant that Alice must indeed have taken Archie with her, wherever she'd gone, and that she didn't want anyone to know where to, or why. She couldn't believe that she had just left with-out telling even her. She loved her and had believed Alice loved her too. Had it all been a sham? Then she realised that wherever she was, she had left in a hurry, taking only a few clothes as though they were going on a short holiday. She checked the cupboards and the fridge and was shocked to find them virtually empty. So why hadn't Alice told her? And why had she taken time off work and kept Archie off school, something she would never normally do?

She had to try to find her but hadn't a clue where to start looking. Of course, she tried ringing Alice but the message just said the number was unobtainable. She realised Her phone must be turned off. Why would she do that? Then she began to wonder what had prompted her to go off like this without a word. It was so out of character. Then, recalling the strange atmosphere in the car after the encounter with the man on the boat, after which Alice had seemed preoccupied all evening, she wondered whether it was something to do with him. At the very least, he might have some idea what was going on. Maybe Archie had mentioned something to him?

She jumped in the car and drove over to the boatyard, enquiring at the office as to which boat was Jack's. She was directed to the Lady Louise. Ben, who was sitting on the rear deck, started barking as she approached, and Jack appeared at the door.

'Oh, hello,' Sam said, 'I'm Sam, Archie's... I mean, I'm Archie's mum's partner.'

'Yes, I saw you last night,' Jack replied. 'Is there a problem?' he went on, dreading the answer he felt was coming.

'They've gone,' Sam announced.

'What do you mean, gone?

'They're not at the house and Alice didn't tell me they were going anywhere, didn't even leave a note. I was wondering whether Archie had said anything to you about a holiday or anything.'

Jack now knew that his worst fears had been

realised, that Archie was Toby, and that he had been taken away from him a second time.

'You'd better come aboard,' he said grimly, 'There are a few things you need to know.'

Jack realised it might be difficult to convince Sam that Alice wasn't the kind of person she had obviously thought she was and didn't quite know where to begin. Eventually, he decided to start where it was usually best to start, at the beginning. Only that way would he build up a complete picture and could only hope that certain parts of it may resonate with Sam's knowledge of Alice and Archie.

When he had finished, Sam remained silent for some moments, then said, predictably,

'This doesn't sound like the person I've been living with for six months,' then, after a pause, 'but in fact I had already realised there was some mystery surrounding Archie. When I suggested we book a holiday in France this summer she said we couldn't, because Archie didn't have a passport, and when I said that wasn't a problem, he could be added on to hers, she quickly changed the subject and never mentioned it again, which I thought was odd.'

'Well, of course, she hasn't got a birth certificate for him, so he wouldn't be able to get a passport,' Jack affirmed.

Sam had also noticed the strawberry birth mark on Archie's back, and now she was sitting opposite Jack, she could definitely see the resemblance. Finally, the fact that Alice had fled with Archie convinced her that Jack was most likely right. Archie is Toby. She was utterly shocked, but at the same time she did love the Alice she had thought she knew, and felt she owed it to her to listen to her explanation, if she could find her.

'She must be in a dreadful state,' she said, 'feeling trapped, not knowing where to turn next. For everyone's sake I have to find her.'

Jack agreed, saying she would be in a dangerous frame of mind. He must find his son. He could be in great danger if she felt cornered. They agreed to keep in touch and exchanged phone numbers, but before Sam left, they decided that Jack should ring DC Jones to update him. The police needed to know that Alice had definitely left and had taken Archie with her.

It turned out they had already been in touch with Tidmouth, who were sending the information across. They had ascertained that Ms Cookson hadn't been in school that day, he said, but they had given him her home address. He had just been round to the house himself, but found no-one in. When Jack said he was with Ms Cookson's partner who had told him they had gone, DC Jones said they would like to speak to her partner and told Jack to ask Sam to call in at the station so that they could take down some details.

***

After Sam left, Jack tried to ring Alice's number, but it was unavailable, and he too realised she must have turned it off. He felt utterly helpless, just as he had on that dreadful day when she had taken Toby away for the first time. He was angry that he was just as powerless to find him. Thoughts of Grace once again crowded into his mind, the sight of her in that bath with her lifeblood drained away and the dreadful feelings of guilt he had borne all these years. But that woman was the one responsible for Grace's death, as surely as if she had slit her wrists for her. Throughout those years that woman had his Toby, watching him grow up, hearing his first words, taking him to his first day at school. Those years were gone forever, but he was determined that whatever it took, Toby's future would be with him.

Chapter Thirteen

Sam drove back to the house and after grabbing a bite to eat, made her way to the police station. When she explained who she was, she was shown into a side room. In a few moments two people entered. They introduced themselves as Detective Inspector Scott and Detective Constable Cotton. They sat down across the table from her.

'Thank you for coming in,' Alex said, in an authoritative tone.

After taking his full details, Alex asked Sam what her relationship was to Ms Alice Cookson and Sam informed her that they had been living together for the past six months. Alex then asked her whether they had a good relationship. Sam was rather taken aback at such a seemingly irrelevant question, but nevertheless quickly replied that yes, it was, very good.

'Isn't it rather strange then, that she should have disappeared without telling you?'

Sam didn't much like the way this was going. It began to dawn on her that if Alice and Archie had disappeared, and if they suspected foul play, she was likely to be in the frame.

Eager to dispell any such suspicions, she replied, 'Yes, it is strange, and until I spoke to Mr Long I had no idea why she might have done so. However, Mr Long has a theory that I know you're familiar with.'

'He has, and of course we are pursuing that line of enquiry, but at this stage we can rule nothing out.'

Sam shifted uncomfortably in her seat, which wasn't lost on Alex, who went on purposefully,

'Well, we will need to visit the house immediately. We need to gather samples of their DNA, and we'll need yours too, for elimination purposes of course. I assume you have no objection?'

'No of course not,' Sam replied quickly, eager to dispel any idea they had in their minds that he had had a hand in their disappearance.

'I assume you have tried to ring Miss Cookson?' DCI Scott asked.

'Of course, but it just says it's unavailable. I imagine she must have switched her phone off.'

DC Cotton made a note of Alice's phone number and the registration number of her car.

At that, it seemed as if the interview was over for the moment and Alex stood up.

'DC Cotton will take you next door, where forensics will take a DNA swab, and then we will accompany you to the house, if you are in agreement.'

'Yes of course,' Sam said, glad that at least they now seemed to be taking this seriously.

When they arrived at the house, the forensic scientist who had accompanied them took various samples; hair from a brush Archie used, Alice's nightdress, and other various pieces they thought may be useful. Alex and Neil Cotton made a thorough search of the house. Sam supposed they were making certain that Alice and Archie were definitely not there. They took away some recent photos of them, presumably, Sam thought, for circulation purposes.

As they were leaving, Alex said,

'We may need to speak to you again of course, and we will keep you updated. Please don't leave the area.'

Sam gave a non-committal reply but as she closed the door, was wondering what she would actually do if Alice rang, or she found out where she was. She supposed the police were thinking the same.

As she lay in bed that night waiting for sleep, her thoughts were of course. full of Alice. From the moment she'd seen her in the staff room on that first day, she knew. Whatever she'd done in the past, and whatever she was doing now, Sam would still love her. She had never felt like this about anyone. She'd had other girlfriends of course, some for casual sex, a few she had thought she'd been in love with for a while, but none of them lasted. She now realised that with all of them the attraction was purely sexual. With Alice it was different. It went much deeper. She now understood what people meant when they said they had met their soulmate. That's exactly how it felt. She made her feel complete. When they made love, it was pure ecstasy, two bodies in perfect harmony.

She had felt she understood her completely, which is why she now felt so devastated, realising there had been a whole area of Alice's life she knew nothing about. Of course, she understood why she had felt unable to share the truth about Archie with her. Sam realised that once she had made the split-second decision outside that shop for whatever reason all those years ago, she must have felt there was absolutely no way back. As of this moment, she had no idea why she had done it, but something profound must have happened to compel her to. It must have been a traumatic event so awful that her mind was disturbed to such an extent that she had lost her grip on reality. Maybe she had lost a child. Sam had heard of such things, when a woman, grieving for the loss of her child had taken someone else's, believing it to be her dead baby.

She felt sure if she had been in a rational state of mind, she could never have done such a thing. She would have understood what a devastating effect it would have on the child's parents. In the event, it had destroyed their lives, literally in the case of the boy's mother.

Whatever the truth of it, Sam knew she would stand by her. If she was to have a chance of any kind of a life going forward, she knew Alice would have to face up to the consequences of what she had done and take her punishment, which may well mean prison. No doubt she would lose Archie and knowing how much he meant to her, that in itself would destroy her. All this was of course, why she'd had to run. She knew only too well what would be ahead of her if she had stayed, and just couldn't face it. Thinking it all through like this, Sam was even more afraid for her, knowing just how desperate she was feeling. She would need her, and she was determined she would be there for her, however things worked out.

***

Back at the station, Alex was mulling over the situation. She was still waiting for the files from Tidmouth to arrive and her training told her not to jump to any conclusions just yet. If Alice Cookson had disappeared with Archie, there was still a possibility of foul play. Jack Long would be desperate to get his son back and may well stop at nothing to do so. First she needed to confirm that he was in fact the boy's father and asked Neil to ring him to ask him to come in for interview and to take a DNA test

Chapter Fourteen

It had been late afternoon when they had pulled up at the Travelodge in Carlisle. Unfortunately, Trixie had to spend the night in the car, which upset Archie hugely, but the hotel wouldn't allow her in. They'd fed her and taken her for a walk in a nearby park, then bedded her down on her blanket they had brought with them. Once again, Archie had again tried to find out where they were going, but Alice repeated that it was to be a surprise, but it was somewhere beautiful that he'd never been to before. Something was nagging Archie. His mum, who was never normally far from her phone, hadn't used it once since they had left home. There had been no phone calls, no alerts, nothing. Surely Sam should have been calling her at the very least. In the end he thought that perhaps she just needed a complete break and had turned it off, but it did seem rather odd.

***

The next morning Alice woke early. Archie was still fast asleep beside her. She began to consider her next move. She had to assume that by now, Sam and Jack

Long would both have realised she had left and taken Archie with her. Jack Long would certainly have contacted the police. She wasn't sure what Sam would have done. Her heart ached at the thought of how she would be feeling, convinced no doubt that she had left her, without a word. Still, there was nothing to be done about that yet. Maybe in the end she would be able to make it up to her, but for the moment she had to put her out of her mind and concentrate on trying to stay ahead of Jack Long, and no doubt the police too. She decided from here onwards she would have to try to avoid the motorways and their CCTV cameras as much as possible. They would be bound to have discovered her car registration number and would soon be on the look-out for her.

Carefully climbing out of bed so as not to disturb Archie, she took the AA road atlas out of her bag. She had to work out a route to the highlands which minimised the risk of her being spotted and decided to take the A7 to Gretna and then stick to the A roads up to Glasgow, via Kilmarnock. From Glasgow she would have to take the A82 along the side of Loch Lomond, hoping the police still wouldn't have realised that she had travelled to Scotland. Taking the Kilmarnock route would add at least another hour to their journey, but she felt it would be the safer option. Making a mental note of the route she put the atlas back in the bottom of her bag.

She showered and dressed then woke Archie up. He immediately wanted to know if she'd been out to check on Trixie. She said she'd only just got dressed, so he should hurry to get himself washed and dressed and they would go down to feed her then get some breakfast themselves. They had quite a way to travel today she told him, then immediately regretted saying that, as he once again began to pester her to find out where they were going. She decided that it was probably safe now to tell him that they were heading for the mountains in Scotland and would be staying in a wonderful place.

'How long are we staying there, mum?' he asked.

'Oh, just a few days,' she replied.

'But mum it seems a long way to go for a few days!'

Pausing briefly before replying, she agreed, 'Well, yes, it is a long way, but it will be good to just get away from everything, won't it? Just the three of us,' carefully including Trixie.

'I suppose so,' Archie admitted.

Satisfied again, for the moment at least, he washed and dressed quickly, by which time Alice had packed their things. They went out to the carpark to check on Trixie. She seemed to have suffered no ill effects from her night spent in the car. They fed her and took her for a walk before returning to the hotel for their own breakfast.

An hour later they were on their way, Alice having topped up the car with petrol at the garage next to the hotel. She knew she had a good six and a half-hour drive ahead of her. At least the weather was good, which would make the drive less arduous.

She turned on the radio, tuning it to Heart, and they settled back to listen to the music as they drove along. Archie still didn't understand why they were travelling so far just for a few days holiday. Grown-ups were strange sometimes, he thought. However, he had decided he might as well enjoy this holiday with his mum and Trixie. It could be fun, and after all, he'd be home again in a few days. He was determined that they would not stop him from seeing Jack and Ben, whatever they had said, and he would be able to tell Jack all about it.

They stopped off at a pub just outside Kilmarnock, where they gave Trixie a break and ate lunch before getting underway again. Alice knew she must now face the drive through Glasgow, a city she was unfamiliar with, and without the satnav it might be tricky, but she couldn't risk turning her phone on. She would just have to follow the signs to Loch Lomond initially and then the Highlands. As far as CCTV cameras were concerned, she just hoped they would have difficulty spotting her in the midst of the busy city traffic. With at least another four hours driving ahead of her they would need to stop on the way. She knew she would be driving through Glencoe, so maybe the visitor cen-tre would be a good option.

After leaving Glasgow behind, and driving north for an hour or so, they arrived on the shores of Loch Lomond and Alice began to relax a little. Now she was away from the motorways and out of sight of the cameras, she was beginning to feel more secure, even daring to look forward to spending time in the Highlands. This was somewhere she had spent many happy holidays with her parents when she still had parents. She hadn't thought about them for years. Not surprising she thought, that they should pop back into her head at this moment; some of the happiest times of her life had been spent among the hills and glens along the west coast of Scotland. Then she quickly decided this wasn't the time for reminiscing. She had more pressing business to consider. She stopped at a garage at the southern end of Loch Lomond, filling the car to the brim with petrol, unsure when she would be passing another petrol station after this point.

So far, she had been preoccupied with putting as many miles between Archie and Jack Long as possible and hadn't given much thought to what might come next. Well, she had done it before; disappeared. For ten years no one had ever suspected anything and if she hadn't moved last year, she may still have kept her secret. So, she reasoned, she would just have to do it again. Of course, with Archie being twelve years old, it wouldn't be quite so simple. He now had a history too and getting him into school for instance, without reference to his previous one might be tricky. Still, one step at a time, she told herself, concentrating once again on the road ahead and the beautiful views across Loch Lomond.

Archie also seemed to be enjoying the scenery. Remembering stories of the battles of the clans her father had told her so many times as they travelled these roads, and as they were soon to pass through Glencoe, she began to tell Archie the story of how the Campbells and the McDonalds had fought a famous battle there. She recounted how the Campbells surprised the McDonalds and massacred many of them simply because they wouldn't swear allegiance to the protestant King George. He listened intently, thrilled that they would soon be travelling through the very spot where it all happened. Other stories came into Alice's mind, and she kept Archie, and herself, entertained until at last they came to the hills of Glencoe, sweeping down majestically to the river Coe at its heart.

It was mid-afternoon now and although they took a break, of necessity it had to be a short one. They still had some hours driving ahead of them. They had coffee and cake, let Trixie out to relieve herself and to give her a drink, and visited the loo. After picking up a book for Archie about the Battle of Glencoe from the Visitor Centre shop, within minutes they were back on the road.

Chapter Fifteen

The DNA tests had been fast tracked and when the results came in the next day it became apparent that Alice Cookson was definitely not Archie's mother. Jack Long had been happy to take a DNA test and after another excruciating twenty-four hours wait, the results were in. It was confirmed beyond any doubt that Archie was, in fact, Toby, and Neil Cotton rang Jack to give him the news. By now Alex had raised the case to 'urgent', sure that Alice Cookson had taken Archie away to avoid investigation into the circumstances of his birth and possible abduction, and that the boy may be in danger.

Alex had been in the force long enough, twenty years in fact, to know that often, the most obvious answer isn't always the right one. There were complicated and possibly dangerous emotions at play in this case. If she was the person who had abducted Toby in Tidmouth, Alice Cookson's world was in danger of tumbling down around her, resulting in her prosecution for the serious crime of child abduction, not to mention losing the boy she had raised as her own for the last ten years. When this story approached its final conclusion as it must, and she felt cornered, what would she do? She couldn't imagine that Alice Cookson would calmly hand over her son. That would be the point of maximum danger to them both. If that's how it ended, it would need careful handling.

Likewise, Jack Long, who had thought his child had gone forever, would have been desperate to have him back once he had decided in his own mind that Archie was in fact his son Toby. Maybe he had confronted Alice and tried to take the boy, resulting in some kind of altercation that didn't end well. Maybe his approach to the police was his attempt to cover something up. Alex determined to take a closer look at Jack Long.

Last but not least there was the girlfriend, Sam Bolton. Just how strong is her relationship to Alice? Would it be strong enough for her to collude with her in taking the boy away, maybe with the intention of staying around to point us in the wrong direction, with a view to joining her when things died down?

Alex called Neil to join her in her office, then told him to call everyone together for a case conference. As of now, she had a core team of four detectives but could pull in other resources to work on the case if needed. Cotton was her 'bagman'. He'd been with her for only six months, and he was young. He was a graduate recruit and had completed his two-year Detective

Training Program just last year. He was keen, sometimes a little too keen, but he was bright and observant. Alex felt he would go far in the force.

DS Sally Nugent was thirty years old. She had a sharp and analytical brain, and was good at working out connections, an invaluable skill in any police work, but particularly in detective work. Sally was married with a four-year-old son. Alex knew how hard it was to manage parental commitments with the demands of the job and did tend to cut her a bit of slack occasionally.

Detective Sergeant Pete Carter had only recently joined the team. He was an experienced officer but seemed to have progressed as far through the ranks as he was destined to go. He was thorough, but what might be termed a 'bit of a plodder'. Pete was the person Alex would go to when painstaking research into records or evidence stores was needed. He was happiest when he had a specific task in hand and he wouldn't give up until he'd got to the bottom of whatever issue needed to be resolved.

Finally, Detective Constable Mark Jones had completed his National Detective Program training and was now in his probationary period. So far, he had impressed Alex with his readiness to undertake routine jobs, but never in a short-sighted way, always with an eye on the bigger picture. He also seemed a bit of a whizz with technology. He would go far, she was sure.

***

All in all, Alex was confident she had a good team

around her. Of course, she had other resources to call on when needed. Her first task, now that she was sure that the boy was in fact Toby, and that he had indeed been taken from Jack Long ten years ago, was to decide whether to instigate a Child Rescue Alert. How would Alice react if she discovered they were searching for her nationwide? Would she panic? The last thing Alex wanted to do was to provoke her into a dangerous course of action.

She decided to discuss it with her boss, Detective Superintendent Colin Davis. He was of course an officer with many years' experience. Alex had always found him to be supportive and ready to listen to her when she needed advice on a particular matter. He could also, unfortunately, be a bit of a stickler when it came to requests for more resources. She knocked on his office door and heard him call 'Enter!'

Alex gave him an update on the case and then explained she just needed a second opinion on whether a Child Rescue Alert should be instigated. After a brief discussion on the circumstances of the case they concluded that in fact, if Ms Cookson had taken the boy, she must already be aware they would be searching for her, that they had her car registration and would be watching CCTV cameras across the country. She would also be aware that they would be circulating their photos and that she would more than likely have gone somewhere isolated anyway. In view of this they decided that, on balance, the CRA should be informed.

Alex also confirmed that of course, her team would put a general alert out for Ms Cookson's car. She added that their photographs would be circulated to the airports and ferry terminals, even though Ms Bolton had told them she didn't believe Ms Cookson had a passport for Archie.

'Of course, Sir,' she went on, 'We'll be keeping all options on the table at this stage.'

'Of course, that's essential. Do you feel you've got enough help at the moment?'

'I do Sir, but that might change of course. I'll keep you informed of progress and any further resources I may need.'

'Very good. Thank you and good luck!'

'Thank you, Sir.'

***

With that, Alex returned to her office to consider the 'options' in more detail before addressing her team. Glancing through the window she could see they had assembled and were waiting for her to brief them on the case, and after a few moments she got up and strode into the outer office.

'OK folks!' she declared. 'Listen up.'

They all turned to face her, and she proceeded to set out the facts of the case, explaining that it was going to be one that would need careful handling.

'We have a twenty-nine-year-old woman, Alice Cookson,' she began, turning to pin the photo of Alice on the evidence board, 'and we also have a twelve-year-old boy, presently known as Archie Cookson, and they both went missing two days ago.'

She handed Archie's photo to Neil Jones who pinned it to the board and joined it to Alice's with tape.

'As of this moment, we are treating it as a missing person's enquiry. However, we are also aware that ten years ago Archie Cookson was abducted from his father Jack Long, in Tidmouth. Toby was never found, and our DNA tests show that Archie is in fact Toby, Mr Long's son. At this stage we have no proof that Alice Cookson was the person who abducted the boy back then, but it does seem a reasonable assumption. It is possible however, that in the intervening years he had been placed into the care system at some point and that Cookson had legitimately been given custody of him through adoption or fostering. Mr Long does seem sure that Cookson was the woman who took him, but people can change a lot in ten years, and he could be mistaken. Of course, if Cookson has run off with the lad, that would imply that she is in fact the person who took him in the first place.

'So, we need to urgently establish the whereabouts of Alice Cookson and the boy. Indeed, is Alice still alive? Is the boy? We have to consider the possibility of foul play here. Apparently, Jack Long had already realised that the boy was probably his son, even before DNA confirmed it. Did he take pre-emptive action to try to get the boy back? Is he hiding the lad somewhere having disposed of his mother? I need to know every-thing there is to know about Jack Long – can you deal with that Pete? Is there anything on him on the data-base – we have his DNA, and I am aware that his wife committed suicide some months after the boy went missing – how safe was the suicide verdict?'

'OK boss, will do,' Pete acknowledged.

'Thanks, then there's the girlfriend, Samantha Bolton. She's been living with Alice and the boy for the last six months, so we need to consider whether she's colluding with her already or may do in the future. She is no doubt aware that if Cookson has run away, it will imply that she is guilty of abducting the lad and if caught will be charged with two counts of abduc-tion, almost certainly meaning a prison sentence, but at the very least, she will be losing the boy she's been raising as her own son. Ms Bolton knows it will prob-ably destroy Cookson. If she is in love with her, she may have decided to help her already, or if she gets in touch with her, may do so in the future. We need to keep a close eye on her until we find Cookson and the boy. In fact, I'd like to have another chat with her. Could you organise that, Mark? Make it tomorrow, if possible, I want to speak to Jack Long first.'

'Yes boss,' Mark Jones replied.

'Sally, once Pete has checked him out, could you bring Jack Long in? I believe he lives on a narrowboat on the canal. While we've got him here, we'll need to take a good look at the boat, so could you liaise with forensics on that?'

'I will boss. Do we know which boat and where it is?'

'Yes we do. Mark, can you give Sally the details, and perhaps you could go along with her to pick Long up?'

Mark Jones indicated that he would.

'We may also need to raise a Child Rescue Alert. Will you get the information together for that Neil? They will need full details and photos etc, but don't action it just yet.'

Neil sprang up from his seat,

'Sure thing boss!' he declared eagerly.

With a wry smile Alex said,

'OK, that's it. A boy's life may be in danger here, whatever has happened to them, we have to find these two urgently, so let's get to it.'

***

Back in her office, Alex decided she should let Dave know that she was now involved in an urgent case and may be home late tonight. She gave him a ring and asked him to make sure the kids got home alright. Johnny was fifteen and Aby thirteen, so they no longer needed to be picked up, but Alex did like to make sure that either she or Dave checked in with them around four thirty to make sure they had arrived home safely. Dave assured her he would take care of it and wished her luck with the case.

'I think we're going to need it,' she told him, 'it's a tricky one this.'

With that, she said she loved him and would get home as soon as she could.

Chapter Sixteen

Within half an hour, Pete Carter had checked the database and located the record relating to Jack's drink driving offence and had also spoken to the DCI in Tidmouth who had been involved both in the abduction of the child and the subsequent suicide of his mother. The abduction case had remained open as the child was never found, in spite of thorough searches and television appeals for information. Regarding Grace Long's death, Jack Long had been questioned at length but in the end it had been concluded that she had indeed committed suicide and no further action was taken.

He passed all this information on to Sally who then, along with Mark made her way to the boatyard, only to find that Jack's boat was no longer there. The manager of the yard told them that he had moved back towards town. To their annoyance, it took another half hour to drive round to the other end of that section of the canal and park up. After a five-minute walk along the towpath, they finally arrived at the Lady Louise.

Jack was dozing on his bed when Ben suddenly jumped up from the rug and started barking.

'What's up boy?' he asked.

There was a loud thumping on the door and Jack sprang out of bed, shouting,

'All right, all right, I'm coming!'

When he opened the door a woman of about thirty was peering down into the boat.

'Jack Long?' she enquired.

Something about her bearing and the tone of voice she used, told him that this was no social call.

'Yes, I'm Jack Long,' he replied.

'DS Nugent,' she stated, showing him her warrant card, 'and this is DC Jones,' she went on, stepping aside slightly so that Jack could see the young detective standing behind her. There was a brief pause, Jack wondering what they wanted.

'Have you some news about my son?'

Sally didn't reply to that, but said, 'DCI Scott would like you to come down to the station to assist us with our enquiries, if you don't mind.'

'How long will that take? As you can see, I have the dog to think about. I can't leave him for too long.'

'Of course, don't worry about the dog. We can take care of that if necessary.'

Jack didn't like the sound of that. 'If necessary!' What did that mean, he wondered.

He was still in his boxer shorts and asked them to wait a minute until he got some clothes on.

He left some food and water for Ben and then closed up the boat and followed the two detectives along the towpath.

'We had a job to find you Mr Long. We were told your boat was at the boatyard.'

'Yes, it was, but the repairs were finished for now, so I brought it back here, which is my usual spot.'

'I see,' Sally replied, with an emphasis that told Jack that she had found this rather suspicious.

***

He was beginning to feel nervous now. Why did they want to question him? He felt he was being treated as a suspect. Perhaps he was just imagining it, he thought. In the last couple of days, he had been in a highly emotional state. It had resurrected memories of the day Toby had been taken and of finding Grace in the bath. He still struggled with feelings of guilt about that. Still blamed himself for allowing that woman to take Toby. Could it be that the police had seen the files about her death? Were they looking at it again, wondering once more if it had actually been suicide? If so, did they now suspect he had something to do with the disappearance of the woman and his son? All this was running through his head as they drove to the police station, so that by the time they arrived there, he already looked nervous, which did nothing to convince Sally Nugent that he was entirely innocent.

Mark Jones showed him into the interview room and shortly afterwards the woman he knew as DCI

Scott entered, followed by DS Nugent and they both sat down opposite him. Sally Nugent switched on the tape recorder and stated who was present.

'Why are you taping this?' Jack asked with a note of alarm.

'Just for the record, Mr Long. It's the usual procedure in a case such as this.'

Realising he couldn't object further without giving the impression he was afraid of saying something that might in some way imply guilt, he stayed silent.

'By the way, we need to inspect your boat Mr Long. I'm sure you understand that at this stage we have to cover all bases.'

'I suppose you have your job to do, but I don't know what you hope to find.'

'Well, as I say, we just have to eliminate possibilities until we get at the truth. Could you give me the keys so that we can get on with it right away?'

'I don't think that's a very good idea, with Ben there. I don't think your team would get very far, he's an effective guard dog.'

'Well, in that case,' Alex said, 'maybe we'll accompany you back there later so that you can deal with the dog.'

Jack shrugged and said, 'I suppose so, if you must.'

Alex went on to say they had received the files from Tidmouth but that they would like to hear his account in his own words. She asked him if he would be kind enough to tell them exactly what had happened when his son Toby, was taken from him, and also the circumstances around the death of his wife, Grace. This was awful. He felt himself shaking with emotion. Why were they dragging all this up? It had nothing to do with what was going on now, and he said as much.

'Well, obviously what happened then may have a huge bearing on the current events around your son Mr Long, and we do have to look at all possibilities.'

Sally was watching him intently, which only served to make him more nervous. He had to fold his hands to stop them trembling, and she missed nothing, he could see that. However, he finally managed to regain control and force himself to go through that dreadful day all over again.

'That must have been horrific for you Mr Long,' Alex said sympathetically. 'Forgive me, but the notes in the file show that your wife blamed you in some way, for the loss of her child? That must have been very hard.'

'It was, but it was a long time ago.'

'So, tell me about your wife's death,' Alex asked, with an open expression and sympathetic smile.

Sally was still scrutinising him, now concentrating on his face. Under her intense gaze, he found himself flushing. Oh my God, he thought, they must think I might have murdered Grace! If so, perhaps they think I'm responsible for that woman's disappearance – and his son?! How could they think he'd hurt his own son?

'Mr Long?' Alex prompted him.

'Err, yes, of course,' he managed, then went on to

explain how he had found her in the bath with her wrists cut. Sally Nugent was rather disconcertingly making the odd note in her notebook.

When he had finished, the interview turned to his relationship with Archie.

'Had you met Archie often, Mr Long?' Sally asked him.

'Quite a few times over the last couple of months,' he replied. 'He liked my dog, Ben.'

'Did his mother know that you'd been seeing him?'

'Apparently not, although I didn't find that out until Sunday. If I had known, I would have insisted he tell her.'

'So, by the time she found out, you'd built up quite a relationship with him?'

'Well, yes, I suppose you could say that.'

'And when did you suspect Archie was your son Toby?'

'I began to seriously suspect it when I saw the birthmark on his back, which was exactly like the one Toby had had.'

'How did you feel when you thought he might be Toby?'

'I was confused. It didn't seem possible, it was too much of a coincidence, and yet, I had always felt an empathy towards him. At first, I tried to dismiss it because, since... since he'd gone missing, I'd tried so hard to put it behind me, that I was afraid to believe it, in case it wasn't true, and I had to endure the loss all over again.'

'I can see that,' Alex interjected, 'so what did you decide to do about it?'

'Well, I didn't say anything to Toby. I realised that if true, the news would have completely turned his life upside down. After all, as far as I knew, he'd been with that woman for ten years. I knew that whatever was done it would have to be done sensitively.'

'So, did you just decide to do nothing about it? That must have been almost impossible.'

'It was, but I had to think about the lad. Of course, I knew that I would somehow have to try to find out once and for all and then to get him back, but that I would need help to do that, and it wasn't something I could just jump into.'

'So, what changed?' Sally asked sharply.

'What changed, was that Archie – Toby – had a row with her and Sam, because he told her he'd been seeing me, and he'd stormed out and turned up at the boat on his bike. I'd moved it to the boatyard and by the time he found me it was nearly dark. He said he wanted to leave home and live with me. I told him he couldn't do that and had to go back to his mother. However, it was nearly dark by then, so we rang her and told her where he was and that they'd have to come and collect him from the boatyard.'

'Why did Ms Cookson not want him to see you?' Alex asked.

'Well, I first saw him about nine months ago and did my best to discourage him, because I prefer my own company. I even moved the boat to the other side of town. Anyway, it turned out that his mother had said she didn't want him talking to strangers on the canal and he wasn't to even ride his bike along there. She had never met me, so it couldn't have been personal. It was after I moved back across town six months later, that the boy turned up again. That was in April of this year.'

'I see, so did they come to collect him on Sunday?'

'They did, and as soon as I saw her, I knew. I knew it was her, I could never have forgotten the face of the woman who had ruined my life. I also saw that she recognised me. Neither of us said anything, but we both knew. I was now certain that Archie was my Toby. He had reluctantly followed Sam who was putting his bike in the boot. She turned on her heels and practically ran to the car and jumped in the front seat. I just stood there, completely shocked, and unable to decide what to do next. They left, and as you know, it was Monday morning when I came in here to tell you what had happened.'

'And how did you find out that she had gone away with the boy?'

'When Sam came round on Monday evening to find out if Toby had said anything to me about going away with his mother.'

'And had he?'

'No, not a word. That's when I rang to let you know that Sam had told me they had disappeared.'

'And you've heard nothing from either of them since?'

'No, of course not, I would tell you if I had. I did try to ring her – Toby had given me her number when I rang her to let her know he was with me – but it said the caller couldn't be reached.'

'When was this?'

'Errr, it would have been after Sam had left on Monday evening.'

'Well, we'll need to borrow your phone if you don't mind Mr Long,' Sally pronounced.

'I will need it back as soon as possible, it's my only means of communication and I need it for job-searching. If I can't prove I'm doing that, I lose my benefits you see.'

Sally looked less than sympathetic but Alex said,

'Of course, we shouldn't need it for more than a day or so. If you wait here, DS Nugent will accompany you back to the boat shortly. We may of course need to speak with you again.'

Sally signed off on the tape and they both left Jack to ponder over what had just happened. He felt he'd given a good account of everything and hoped that even though they were 'covering all bases' as the detective had said, they were also concentrating on actually trying to find Toby.

***

When they arrived at the boat Sally said that, along with the forensics officer who had accompanied them they would need an hour or so to go over the boat, so it might be as well if Jack took Ben off for a walk. After attaching Ben's lead, he left them to it. They carried out a thorough search of the boat, rummaging through the cupboards, checking the underbed storage and the lockers over the windows. No one was sure what they were looking for, but it had to be done. They dusted for fingerprints here and there as they saw fit. The only thing of interest was a tee shirt with paint stains on it. When Jack returned with Ben, Sally asked him whether it had belonged to Archie.

'If you mean Toby, yes, it was just a cheap one I bought from the charity shop for him to use when he did a bit of painting with me sometimes.'

It was bagged up and taken away. After Sally was satisfied they had checked everything, they prepared to leave.

'Thank you for your trouble, Mr Long, we'll leave you in peace. We have made a bit of a mess dusting for fingerprints, but it is unavoidable I'm afraid.'

'So I see,' Jack agreed, then went on, 'so what happens now? I hope you'll be putting out a nationwide alert, they could be anywhere by now.'

'We will keep you informed of any developments Mr Long. We may need to speak to you again. Please inform us if you decide to move your boat again, will you?'

'I will,' Jack agreed, 'but when can I collect my phone? I really do need it. I'm pretty isolated here on the canal.'

'Yes, I can see that. If you call in tomorrow, I'll try to arrange for it to be ready for you.'

With that, they departed, leaving Jack with the

uncomfortable feeling that he was still very much under suspicion.

Chapter Seventeen

As they arrived back at the station, Alex grabbed her coat and instructed Mark Jones to follow her. The thought had occurred to her that she needed to take another look at the Cookson house. Sam Bolton would be at work, but she had obligingly given them a spare key. She wanted to pick up Cookson's laptop if there was one, and any documents they could find. She needed to know more about her background. Had she gone to stay with family? Or perhaps a friend? In addition, it was probable that if she had taken Toby ten years ago, she may have changed her name afterwards to avoid being traced. Alex needed to find anything that would give them her original name.

Mark eagerly jumped into the driving seat. Alex asked him how he was settling in. He said he was enjoying it and everyone had made him welcome. He told her he had contacted Ms Bolton earlier and she had agreed to come in when she'd finished work later that day.

'That's good, maybe after looking through the house we'll have more questions for her.'

***

Five minutes later they arrived at the house. As they got out and strode up the path, Alex made a mental note of a slight movement of the curtains in the house next door. She knew that neighbours, especially nosey ones, could be a great source of information. As a precaution they put on rubber gloves and she unlocked the door. Sending Mark upstairs, she instructed him to look for any laptops or phones, and any leaflets or brochures that may give them a clue where they might be heading. They also needed to find any old document files that might contain references to a previous name. While Mark headed off up to the bedrooms Alex tackled the downstairs rooms.

There was a desk in the corner of the dining room, and she quickly opened each drawer in turn, checking the contents thoroughly for anything that might be helpful. There was an address book, a few current utility bills, some older ones which had Cookson's previous address on them, and a pile of bank and credit card statements. She placed them all into an evidence bag. Apart from these items there was just the usual stationery paraphernalia to be found in the average desk.

Going through into the kitchen she picked up a couple of unopened envelopes from the table. One looked as though it was from the council, probably a Council Tax bill, and the other was a circular from the local Liberal Party. She added these to her previous document haul.

In the corner of the lounge was a large cage which had obviously housed the family dog. She made a note to ask about that. So far no one had mentioned a dog. That might be significant. There were several framed photos around the place, mainly in the lounge. She noted they were all of Ms Cookson and the boy, except one of them that looked more recent. It was of Sam Bolton, Archie and a blond Labrador, so that answered one mystery. There were no photos of the boy as a baby. On one of them he looked to be about three years old. All of this seemed to be corroborating what Alex suspected was the truth, that Cookson was the person who had taken him as a toddler ten years ago.

She called up to Mark to ask if he'd found anything.

'No laptop Boss. If she had one, she must have taken it with her,' he shouted. 'There are a couple of files of documents. I've had a look through them, but I can't find anything with a different surname, so far at any rate.'

Alex climbed the stairs and as she did so, noticed a trapdoor to the loft. That's definitely worth a look, she thought. If Cookson had hidden anything from Sam Bolton, or indeed, from the boy, that's probably where we'll find it.

'Mark, we need to take a look at this. Go and see if there's a stepladder anywhere – in the garage probably. There's a garage key on this ring,' she told him, handing him the keys as he came out onto the landing, glancing up at the trapdoor.

'I had noticed that and wondered myself. I'll go and

see what I can find,' he said, hurrying down the stairs and out of the front door.

Alex popped her head into each room in turn while she waited for him to come back. There were three bedrooms and the bathroom. One was obviously the boy's room. It was full of the usual posters of footballers, a map, dinosaurs, and superheroes to be found in any twelve-year-old boy's room. She was surprised to see that the bed was in disarray. The larger of the other bedrooms was in a similar state while the rest of the house had seemed very tidy, and she had concluded that the lady who lived here liked things to be that way. Did she leave in a hurry? She checked the wardrobe and the drawers. There were clothes, but she concluded that they wouldn't have been able to take everything anyway and would just have taken essentials with them. The third, small bedroom was quite tidy with an uncovered duvet pulled up neatly on the single bed, this room seemingly unused apart from storing a few boxes of books.

At that moment she heard Mark on the landing. He had found some stepladders and was now placing them under the trapdoor.

'Up you go then, Constable,' Alex urged him with a smile. 'Let's see what we can find.'

With some difficulty, as the stepladder wasn't really high enough, he eventually managed to push the trapdoor aside and pull himself up into the opening. Taking out his phone he turned on the torch app and took a look around. There wasn't much there. Just a couple of open-topped boxes full of arch lever files that looked like a legacy from some sort of a study course. He checked them and found that they were from a teacher training course and the name on them was Alice Cookson. He called down to Alex to ask her whether she wanted him to pass them down, but she said as long as they were in her current name they could be left where they were. She knew where they were if they needed to be looked into further. There was also an old leather brief case that looked a little more interesting, which he passed down to Alex.

When she opened it she took out a file which contained documents in plastic pockets,

'Bingo! These are her qualifications from school Mark, and in the name of Alice Whitehead. Not only that, there's a school photo or two from Blaketown Road Comprehensive in Bristol.'

'That sounds promising,' Mark called down to her. 'Do you need anything else from up here?'

'Not at the moment, so you can come down now.'

While Alex held the ladder, he sat for a moment with his legs dangling from the opening, then eased himself down onto the top of the stepladder, closing the trapdoor before clambering down, looking rather pleased with himself.

'Okay, we'll take this briefcase with us and I think we're done here. Let's go,' Alex said.

'Okay Boss,' Mark replied, then carried the step-ladders down the stairs and out of the front door. He put them back in the garage, locking the door, by which time Alex was waiting for the keys by the front door. As she was locking up the house, she said,

'Just hang on a minute, I think we'll just check with next door while we're here. They may have seen something.'

She knocked on the front door and a middle-aged woman answered.

'Good afternoon, madam,' she said, 'I'm Detective Inspector Scott, and this is Detective Constable Jones. I wonder if we may come in? I've just got a couple of questions I'd like to ask you.'

'About next door, I suppose? Well, yes, you'd better come in.'

The woman showed them through into the lounge.

'Please, sit down,' she invited them.

'Thank you,' Alex responded pleasantly, 'Mrs ....'

'I'm Maria Blackstone. How can I help?'

Mark took out his notebook and pencil, ready to capture anything of interest.

'Well, it appears that Ms Cookson and Archie have disappeared without letting anyone know and we are rather concerned about them. I was wondering whether you might have noticed anything unusual going on next door?'

'I see. Well, I did notice yesterday morning, that Alice – Ms Cookson – and the boy were loading up the car as though they were going away. I thought it was a bit odd as I know the schools aren't on holiday yet. Then I thought maybe she's been called away urgently, to a sick relative or something. You never know, do you? I did notice that her friend had already gone off to work, so she wasn't with them.'

'What time was this Mrs Blackstone?'

'Well, it would have been about ten o'clock. I know because Woman's Hour had just come on the radio.'

'Have you known Ms Cookson long?'

'Well, they moved in about nine months ago.'

'And how did you get on with her?'

'Well, I didn't have much to do with her to be honest. She didn't seem the type to be neighbouring if you know what I mean. In fact, when they first came, I did try to be friendly, but she soon made it clear she wasn't interested.'

'I see,' Alex went on, 'and what about the boy?'

'He always seemed happy enough, particularly with his dog. I didn't think their landlord let people have dogs, but perhaps they hadn't even asked him. Maybe he found out and they had to leave. They were renting, you know. Renters never stay long, do they? So, I'm not surprised if she's done a bunk.'

'Well, we're not sure what has happened yet, so perhaps we all need to keep an open mind.'

Alex stood up, and sharp as a tack, Mark realised the interview was over, folded his notebook and popped it in his top pocket, then joined his boss in the doorway.

'Thank you so much Mrs Blackstone, you've been a great help.'

'Have I?' Mrs Blackstone beamed.

Alex took out a business card and handed it to her,

asking her to give her a ring if she remembered anything else.

Mrs Blackstone eagerly said that she would and
still smiling, showed them out, obviously pleased that
for once, she had been of use to someone.

Chapter Eighteen

Alex called her troops to attention to review the results of their enquiries so far.

'Sally,' she asked, 'How did you get on with Jack Long? Anything interesting at the boat?'

'Not really,' Sally replied, 'Apart from a tee shirt the boy had obviously been using to paint in, so he had definitely been used to going there.'

'Pete, did you find out anything of interest about Long?'

'Apart from a drink driving offence through which I imagine he lost his job, as he was driving a Post Office van at the time. Probably explains why he lives on a boat. His wife Grace did commit suicide after suffering depression after the loss of her son, Toby. He was questioned at length but in the end Tidmouth were satisfied that she had committed suicide.'

'Thanks Pete. Now, when we visited the house this morning, we discovered that Cookson had indeed changed her name. Whether officially or not I don't know, but she certainly stopped using Whitehead and started calling herself Cookson. Pete, we need to find any relatives, parents, siblings etc and by the way, there were school photos from Blaketown Road Comprehensive, so that might offer a lead or two. Can you get onto it straight away. It's possible she may have taken the lad to her parent's place, so we need to find them pronto and pay them a visit, without alerting them, of course. Also, can we get a monitor on Cookson's phone? Apparently, she had turned it off yesterday, but we need to know if she switches it back on so we can get some indication of her position. Can you deal with that as well Pete?'

'Right Boss, I'll get right onto it,' he assured her.

'While Mark and I were at the house we spoke to the neighbour Mrs Blackstone, who proved to have nothing better to do than to helpfully watch what was going on next door. She had observed Ms Cookson and the boy leaving around 10 am – just the two of them, by the way - having loaded the vehicle with luggage as though they were going away for a while, so it looks as though we can rule out the possibility that they have been abducted. Now, have we had any sightings of the vehicle, Mark? I assume you've checked with traffic?'

'I just called them, they haven't found anything yet, and they said unless we can give them a clue as to where she might be heading, it could take some time.'

'Right, well, if we can find her parents, maybe they'll come up with some suggestions. Now, I believe Sam Bolton is coming in shortly, isn't that right Mark?'

'Yes, she said she should be here by 4.30.'

'OK, Sally, you're with me for that one.'

'Sure Boss,' Sally responded quickly. 'We also need to keep an eye on forensics in case they found anything of interest on the boat.'

'Right, Neil, can you follow that up, tell them it's urgent.'

'OK Boss, will do.'

'Well, I think that's about it for now. Let's see what we get from Ms Bolton and the lab and we'll regroup in the morning, 8am sharp please. Pete, if you've got anywhere with the parents by tomorrow, I'll want to follow it up right away. Hopefully they may still be in the Bristol area, which would make life somewhat easier.'

At that moment a uniformed policewoman called out to Alex that Ms Bolton had arrived and was in reception.

'Thanks PC Dodds,' Alex replied, 'please show her into Interview Room Two.'

'Yes, Ma'am,' the young PC replied and hurried off to carry out the order.

Alex and Sally found Sam Bolton sitting nervously in front of the table in the Interview Room.

Sally turned on the recorder and set up the tape, glancing at Sam, who was shifting uneasily in her chair.

Why does everyone involved in this case seem nervous, Sally thought to herself, completely oblivious to the effect her penetrating gaze had on even the most innocent of interviewees. Alex, on the other hand, had no doubt, born from experience, that having Sally

Nugent in the room often loosened the tongue of the most reluctant respondent.

'Thank you for coming in Ms Bolton,' Alex said, then went on, 'Now, if you've been home, you may have noticed that we visited the house today. I needed to try to find out whether Ms Cookson had ever been known by a different name.'

'I realised that you had been in. Did you find anything helpful?'

'Have you ever heard the name Whitehead mentioned?'

'No, I haven't.'

'Well, it seems that Ms Cookson was once Alice Whitehead, apparently living in Bristol. Did she never talk about her parents?'

Sam sat back, obviously quite taken aback at this news about the woman she thought she had known so well.

'Not really,' Sam replied, 'except she implied that they were no longer around, by which I thought she meant they had died, but she always changed the subject whenever it came up, so I thought that maybe it was difficult for her and didn't pursue it.'

'Didn't Archie ever mention his grandparents, or maybe other relations, aunts, uncles, cousins or the like?'

'Never, which when I come to think about it, is a bit odd.'

Sally Nugent sat forward, leaning her forearms on the table looking directly at Sam, before asking,

'Did Ms Cookson give you any indication that she was going to leave? Had she said anything in the previous few days? Perhaps she mentioned a certain place she hoped to visit?'

'No,' Sam replied, 'absolutely not! She had given no indication at all, except ...'

'Yes?' Alex prompted.

'Well, after we picked Archie up from the boatyard, she seemed ... different.'

'Different?' Sally asked. 'In what way different.'

'She was very quiet, hardly said a word. She didn't even have a go at Archie for going off like that, or for being with Long for that matter. It was all very odd. And when we got back home, she just made some excuse and went to bed early, even though we had intended to go out for a meal that evening.'

'So, in your opinion Ms Bolton, seeing Jack Long prompted an unexpected reaction?'

'Well, it certainly seemed to, which is why I went round to see him, to find out if he knew anything. That was when Mr Long told you she had left.'

'Has she been in touch with you since she left? Think carefully Ms Bolton, before you answer,' queried Sally in a rather accusing tone.

Sam bridled at that, 'I don't need to think carefully, of course she hasn't, I would have told you if she had.'

'By the way,' Sally continued, 'we may well be raising a Child Rescue Alert shortly, so you may see reference to it on the TV. Also, we may need to ask you to do an appeal. Would you be willing to do that?'

'Yes, of course,' Sam answered. 'I'm happy to do anything to help find her.'

'One last thing Ms Bolton, have you ever heard either Ms Cookson or Archie refer to his father?'

'No, never, although I'm sure Archie missed having a dad around, that's probably why he was drawn to Long, I suppose.'

'How was his relationship to you?' Sally asked pointedly.

'It was ok, but I do think that sometimes he resented me, being so close to his mother, I mean. They had apparently been on their own for so long, I think he may have felt a little abandoned by Alice when I came on the scene.'

'Well, I think that's about all for now Ms Bolton,' Alex announced as she pushed back her chair and stood up. 'Please don't leave the area, we may need to speak to you again.'

Sam mumbled her acquiescence then got to her feet, pleased that this was over.

Then Sally spoke up once again,

'Oh, by the way, if Ms Cookson does get in touch, you'll be sure to let us know?'

'Of course,' Sam replied curtly.

'Interview ended 17.00 hours.' Sally signed off on the tape.

After Sam had left, Alex and Sally discussed the interview.

'What did you make of that?' Alex asked her.

'Not sure,' Sally replied. 'She seemed rather nervous

at first, but otherwise, what she said sounded genuine. I think that until now she's played it by the book. However, that may change if Cookson gets in touch with her.'

'I agree, we need to keep a close eye on her in case she makes a move to join her. We need to bring in a surveillance team to keep a 24-hour watch for the moment, can you arrange that Sally? Tomorrow, I'm hoping Pete will have tracked down Cookson's parents and I intend to visit them. Even if she isn't there, they may have an inkling where she might have gone to.'

Sally went off to organise the surveillance and Alex made sure the rest of the team were on track with the tasks she'd given them. There wasn't anything more she could do tonight but hopefully, tomorrow things may start to come together she thought, before grabbing her coat and heading for the door.

As she drove home, she found herself thinking about the case, which she was finding particularly difficult. She couldn't imagine what Jack Long must be going through, losing his son not once, but twice! She swore to herself she wouldn't rest until she had found the boy and returned him to his father. Of course, she could do nothing for his poor mother. What a pity they hadn't been able to find the boy all those years ago. What a tragedy that had been, which made her even more determined that this time they would succeed in bringing him home.

Chapter Nineteen

The next day Alex arrived at the station, determined that today, she would at least find out where Cookson had taken the boy.

'Case conference at eight-thirty sharp,' she called out, to anyone who was in the office, knowing that word would get around to the others.

She had half an hour to consider her next move. She desperately hoped Pete would have been able to find an address for Cookson's parents. If it was in Bristol, as she hoped, she would take Neil with her to find out whether they had heard from their daughter or have any suggestions as to where she might be.

In her own mind she was now satisfied that Jack Long had not had a hand in their disappearance. For a start, he wouldn't have had any opportunity to take them. Sam had been there all night with Cookson and had left her only to go to work on Monday morning. Also, Mrs Blackstone had seen Cookson and the boy loading up the car and leaving the house at ten o'clock with no sign of anyone else around.

She was, however, still unsure about Sam Bolton. She didn't suspect her of being involved so far in their disappearance, but given her obvious feelings for Cookson, Alex couldn't rule out the possibility that she may decide to go to her if she got in touch. In fact, this may turn out to be the best chance they had of finding them.

She got herself a coffee and stood in front of her team, ready to review the previous day's activities, to sum up where they'd got to, and to propose their next steps. She was pleased to hear Pete say that he now had a current address for Mr and Mrs Whitehead, and they were indeed living in Bristol. Alex told Neil that he would be going with her to speak to them. It may even prove to be the end of their search, if Cookson had fled to the family home. Standing a little taller, Neil seemed pleased to be going with Alex. She always treated him with respect, even though he was only a rookie.

'Okay Sally, could you finalise arrangements for the media appeal. Of course, her parents may be willing to do it, and we should know that later today. Failing that, you'll have to ask Sam Bolton. Arrange it for to-morrow and I'll let you know about the parents later.

'Yes Boss,' Sally replied.

'Mark, any news on the cameras yet?'

'There was one possible sighting on the M4 heading west, but the image wasn't good, so we can't be sure it was them.'

'Well, keep on it. Can you make sure we get plenty of copies of the photos of Cookson and the boy ready for distribution by the way?'

'Yes boss.'

'So, what are we thinking? As far as I'm concerned, I'm happy to rule out any involvement of Jack Long in the disappearance. He had neither the opportunity nor the means to take them anywhere. In addition, as Mrs Blackstone saw them leaving alone at ten, long after Sam Bolton had left for work, I think we can rule her out too. However, I do still feel it likely that if Cookson should contact her and ask her to go to her, Bolton may decide to follow, so we need to keep up a keen surveillance on her. We also need to listen in on her phone. Of course, Cookson may use an encrypted message, so we can't assume that we will definitely know if she does make contact. Anybody got anything to add?'

No one actually spoke but there were a few mumbled denials, so Alex assumed they were more or less in agreement.

'Sally, do we have all the resources we need for the surveillance team?'

'Well, as long as she stays put, yes, but if we have to pursue her, we'll need additional resources.'

'Right, well, keep me posted,' Alex went on, 'if we need anything else I'll speak to the Chief Super.

'Pete, in the stuff we retrieved from the house, there are some bills with her previous address on and some bank statements. Could you do some digging to find out any further previous addresses, and also get on to the banks and credit card companies. She must be spending money and we need to know when and where she's using any cards or accounts. I want to know everything there is to know about Alice Cookson, or Alice Whitehead.'

'Will do, Boss,' Pete agreed.

'Each day that passes gives her time to get further away. At least without a passport she can't take him overseas, but the UK is still a big country with plenty of wild places where someone could get lost if they wanted to. We don't really know what this woman's capable of if she feels cornered, and time may be running out, so let's get stuck in. Well, that's all for now,' Alex went on, 'but Neil and I will be out of the office most of the day, so Sally, keep me informed of any developments and we'll reconvene when we get back this afternoon.'

***

It was an hour and a half later that Neil pulled the car up outside a neatly kept semi in Kingsway, Bristol. There was a tidy Ford Escort standing in the driveway. As she got out of the car, Alex felt sorry that she may have to disturb this neat suburban world. Cookson's parents would probably have no idea what was about to hit them, and even she didn't realise just how much the news she brought would turn their world upside down.

She rang the doorbell and after a few moments, a man about sixty years old opened it.

'Hello,' Alex said, 'Mr Whitehead?'

To which he said rather guardedly, 'Yes, I am.'

'Well, I wonder if we might have a word?' Alex continued, as she produced her warrant card and held it out for him to see. 'I'm Detective Inspector Alex Scott and this is Detective Constable Neil Cotton.'

'What's this about?' he enquired, looking rather apprehensive.

Funny how people always seem to react like that at first, Alex thought.

'Do you think we could come in sir?'

'Well, yes, I suppose you'd better,' Mr Whitehead replied, then gestured for them to follow him into the lounge.

Mrs Whitehead was sitting in an armchair, watching television. She looked rather surprised to see two absolute strangers striding into her lounge. Mr Whitehead turned off the television then explained to his wife that they were detectives, who wanted a word with them. He invited them to sit down on the sofa. Neil diligently took out his notebook, pen poised in his hand.

'I'm sorry to land on you like this, unannounced,' said Alex, 'but we needed to speak with you urgently.'

Mrs Whitehead immediately jumped up out of the chair declaring, 'Why, what's happened, is it our son? Has he been in an accident?'

'No,' Alex replied, 'it's not your son. It's about your daughter, Alice. When did you last speak to her?'

From the expressions on their faces, this was the

last thing in the world they were expecting her to say. That much was obvious. Mr Whitehead, after glancing at his wife, finally managed,

'She walked out of here eleven years ago and we've seen and heard nothing of her since that day.'

'I think you need to sit down, as I do have quite a bit of news of her.'

'Well, I for one don't want to hear it,' Mr Whitehead declared. 'After what she put us through! We gave her up for dead years ago.'

'Did you report her as missing, Mr Whitehead?'

'No need,' he replied, 'she left a very explicit note making it clear that she was going and wanted nothing more to do with us, and that was that, we never heard another thing.'

Mrs Whitehead looked on the point of saying something, but then looked at her husband and obviously thought better of it.

Alex ploughed on, 'Well, there may have been a reason why she never contacted you again.'

'What possible reason could there be? She must have known how we would be worrying about her, and she never even contacted her brother Christopher either, even though they were close growing up.'

'Unfortunately, it's probable that shortly after leaving here she did something which meant that she had no way back to this previous life.'

'What on earth do you mean?!' Mrs Whitehead exclaimed. 'Did she commit a crime or something?'

'Well, apparently, and I stress none of this has yet

been proved, she abducted a little boy from his father and has been bringing him up as her own for the past ten years.'

Alex paused, to let that sink in.

'What!! I can't believe that. But after what she'd been through...' her mother declared, shooting an accusing glance at her husband. He looked uncomfortable to say the least.

'What do you mean, Mrs Whitehead, what she'd been through?' Alex queried.

'It's not relevant,' her husband said quickly, 'that was years ago.'

'So was the initial abduction Mr Whitehead, and I'm afraid that we have to be the judge of what is, or is not relevant. Mrs Whitehead, what did you mean?'

'Jack, we have to tell them. If she did this soon after she left us, it may well explain why.'

Without waiting for a response from her husband, she went on,

'When she was sixteen, Alice had a brief relationship with a boy in her class, and unfortunately she became pregnant. We arranged for her to stay in a maternity home to have the baby. We felt she was far too young to have and bring up a child, as did everyone else we spoke to, and in the end it was decided the child would be put up for adoption.'

Here Mrs Whitehead paused, obviously very upset. Mr Whitehead still didn't speak. He was looking down at his feet. Eventually, she began again,

'You'll never know how often I've regretted that

decision. Over the years I have realised what a cruel thing that was. After that she changed, grew apart from us, and the fact that she left and has never returned told me just how much it must have hurt her. You must understand, we thought we were doing it for the best, but we were wrong.'

Finally, Mr Whitehead spoke up, 'You said 'initial abduction'? Has there been another?'

'Well, approximately nine months ago when Archie – that's what she calls the boy, although his original name was Toby – by chance, met his birth father who lives on a narrowboat on the canal less than a mile away from where your daughter was living. When your daughter saw him for the first time, they recognised each other immediately.'

'Oh my God,' interjected Mrs Whitehead, 'you're going to tell us that she's disappeared with the boy again.'

'Unfortunately, yes, it appears so.'

'When was this?' a stern-faced Mr Whitehead enquired.

'Monday last,' Alex told them, 'three days ago. I don't need to tell you that we must find your daughter urgently. We can only imagine what state of mind she's in.'

'Of course,' Mrs Whitehead agreed, obviously feeling very emotional. Not surprising when she had just discovered that her daughter had abducted a child from its parents, not once, but twice!

Suddenly she asked, 'What about the child's mother?'

'Unfortunately, Mrs Whitehead, she took her own life some months after the first abduction.'

Her husband, who so far had seemed impervious to the situation, mumbled 'Oh no!' and put his head in his hands, utterly shocked at the consequences of the action they had taken all those years ago.

'But honestly,' Mrs Whitehead went on, 'I don't know how we can help, as we haven't been part of her life for the last decade.'

'Well, you may be able to. In my experience if someone is trying to find sanctuary, they will often look for it somewhere that had meant something to them. Maybe a place where they had once been happy. Was there any special place for Alice, or a person she may feel she can turn to when she's in trouble?'

'Well,' Mrs Whitehead said thoughtfully, 'I can't think of anyone she would go to. Obviously, she won't come here and her grandparents are all dead. As for friends, I have no idea who they would be after all this time.'

'I can see that,' Alex agreed, then turned to Mr Whitehead asking, 'Is there any particular place you can think of, sir?'

Mr Whitehead looked up, and with a slight shake of his head was obviously trying to clear his mind of the terrible information he'd just been given. After a brief pause, he looked at his wife and declared,

'What about the cottage?'

'Yes! That's possible, she always loved it there!' she replied.

'What cottage is this?' Alex enquired.

Mr Whitehead went on, 'Every year when the children were little, we used to take a holiday in Scotland. We would stay at a cottage near Fort William. Alice was always happy to spend time there. If there is anywhere she might head to, that could be it.'

'We'll follow that up of course. Do you still have any details about it?'

'I believe so,' he said, 'I'll go and look.'

With that, he left the room, returning a couple of minutes later with an arch lever file full of correspondence, obviously all filed neatly in date order, and in no time at all he located the letter confirming a booking twenty years earlier.

'Yes, here it is,' he said triumphantly, handing the sheet of paper to Alex.

'Well, that's quite a long time ago, but we will certainly check it out.'

Handing it to Neil, she went on, 'Can you think of anywhere else?'

'I'm afraid not, can you Mary?' he asked his wife.

She shook her head then asked whether Alex had a partner. Alex told her that it was a Samantha Bolton, and Mary Whitehead looked a little shocked at the mention of Ms Bolton. She explained that they were both schoolteachers and at this point her eyes filled with tears, perhaps, Alex thought because she had realised that her daughter had tried to make something of her life, in spite of the horrendous mistake she'd made all those years ago.

'Can I ask you to let us know when you do find her, Inspector? She may need us more than ever, to face what is ahead of her.'

'Of course,' Alex assured her.

She took out her card and handed it to Mr White-head.

'If she does try to contact you at all, please let me know. It's in everyone's interest, not least Alice's, that she's found, and the boy brought home and returned safely to his father as soon as possible.'

Mr Whitehead took the card, but it was his wife who spoke,

'Of course we will, Inspector.'

Alex stood up to go. Neil closed his notebook folding the letter about the cottage inside, then got up and followed his boss to the front door.

'Well, thank you for your time and we'll be in touch as soon as we hear anything,' Alex said,

'Thank you,' they both replied almost in unison.

Back in the car, Alex had asked Neil for the letter and as they drove along, she called the office and spoke to Pete. Giving him the details, she told him to try to track down the owners of the cottage, to find out if anyone was staying there at the moment or was booked in to take it in the near future, and for how long.

She also spoke to Sally telling her that she had decided to hold off on the media appeal for the moment and told her to ask Mark to ask Traffic to check out any cameras along the M4, M5 and M6 routes to Scotland, and then to liaise with the Scottish police for them to check the routes to the cottage, the address of which she had just given to Pete, as there was a chance she would be heading there. As Cookson's parents wouldn't be doing the appeal, that just left Sam Bolton and she didn't want to spook her right now. If Cookson contacted her, she was pretty sure she would go to her and if so, would lead them directly to her. She wanted to keep that possibility open in case she was wrong about the cottage in Scotland.

Chapter Twenty

Jack had hardly slept since Sunday. The recent events had awakened all the horror of those days and weeks in Tidmouth. The overpowering sense of guilt. Guilt for letting his little boy down, by allowing a perfect stranger to simply walk off with him, and the realisation that as a result of his negligence, his son had lost his mother, and unable to live with the loss of her son, his wife had lost her life. He thought he'd buried all this too deep to ever be felt again, but now it seemed like only yesterday he'd stepped outside that shop, to find Toby gone. The pain of remembering that moment cut through him like a knife.

His every instinct was telling him he had to go and find his son, exactly as he had kept on trying to do all those years ago. He had tramped the streets day after day, in every spare moment he could find, searching, always searching, peering at faces trying to spot the one face, the face of that woman who he was sure had taken his son from him. Now of course, he knew that he had found that face, and she still had his son, his Toby, and now he had allowed her to take him again, before he even had a chance to tell him that he is his father. It was just too cruel.

He had to find out where she'd gone. But how? He had no resources, little money, no transport apart from the boat which was hardly suited to a high-speed chase! He had collected his phone from the station and called her number several times in the hope that she, or even Toby, might answer it, all to no avail. However, he was a little disconcerted when they mentioned putting out an appeal in the media. Of course, he couldn't take part in it. If he had appeared just as a friend of the boy, it may spook Ms Cookson into even more reckless behaviour. He assumed it would be Sam who was put up for the job. He gradually came to the realisation he was going to have to leave it to the police, hoping to God they found them before desperation drove her to do something too awful to contemplate.

In the end, he turned to his main source of solace, painting. He had a photo of Toby and Trixie he'd taken only the week before and decided he would paint it for Toby for when he returned. As he painted, he was able to focus on the face of his son, registering every line, every feature, and as he did so, he began to believe that he would see him again. This painting was for him, and he would return, he must. The police still seemed optimistic of tracking them down, although they didn't tell him much when he rang for an update. He realised it was probably just standard practice to keep reassuring relatives with platitudes. As he was more or less powerless to do anything though, he knew he had no option but to put his trust in them to do their jobs and bring his son safely back to him.

There was one other thing he could do though. He would sell the boat. He couldn't have Toby living here, and he would need money to put down either as a deposit on a rented place, or he wondered whether he could raise enough to buy a mobile home in the area. He knew there were some two-bedroom ones in the site on the outskirts of town. One of those will be perfect for the two of us he thought. He rang the 'Canal Boat' magazine and placed an advert in 'boats for sale'.

***

Less than two miles away, Sam was going through her own version of hell. Alice was everything she had always wanted, needed. She had thought Alice would be her life-partner and had decided to ask her to marry her. She had been going to do it that very night, the night everything changed. Now she had gone, not only physically departed, but she realised that the woman she loved had a whole other persona. She wasn't even Alice Cookson. She was Alice Whitehead.

She had thought she knew Alice so well. Now she felt she hardly knew her at all. And yet, she couldn't believe what they had had was a complete sham. She had felt the love, sensed her basic goodness, believed in her integrity. Surely it wasn't all an act? She'd observed her at school, working hard with her pupils, trying to ensure they all reached their true potential, even the ones who struggled academically. In spite of everything she had learnt recently, she realised she still loved Alice deeply.

She too, tried to ring her several times during the day, desperate to hear her voice. She wondered what she would do if she did answer, and she was able to find out where they were. Would she tell the police? She was genuinely in a quandary. She knew she should help them to find her, but when they did, she would be arrested, and Archie taken from her. Would she be able to survive that? It could destroy her. But what she had done had been wrong and had resulted in the ruination of Jack Long's life and the death of his wife, not to mention depriving the lad of his mother and father. Her natural sense of justice told her that someone ought to pay for all that, and that the lad ought to be returned to his father.

She remained in this state of indecision which was tormenting her day and night. She genuinely had no idea how she would react if Alice contacted her. In the end she decided that in the event she would just have to follow her instincts.

She tried to concentrate on work. Kids still needed educating, she told herself, although it was difficult not to be distracted by thoughts of Alice, wondering where on earth she could be. That didn't stop her making contingency plans. She made sure that the car was topped up with petrol and had a bag packed with clothes, her passport, and other essentials, just in case she should call her. She also had a letter prepared that she would post to school to explain that she'd had to go away on urgent family business and would be in touch again as soon as possible. Although she'd completed her plans she still hadn't made up her mind. If Alice called and asked her to go to her, would she? She just had to wait for her call and then make her decision.

Chapter Twenty-One

When Alex and Neil arrived back at the Station, the team were ready to give them a rundown of the day's progress. Pete had discovered there was no longer a holiday cottage at the address Alex had given him earlier. She now handed him the actual letter, which had the name of the owner, and a holiday rental hub website, and Pete went off to see if he could find anything about the owners themselves. He thought It was possible it was now advertised under a different website, or maybe it was now a private house rather than a holiday cottage.

Mark had had more luck with his enquiries about the motorway CCTV's. There had been a sighting of the car on the M6, heading north at 3.30 pm on Monday. He hadn't yet had time to contact the Fort William police, and Alex asked him to get on to it right away, but not to actually give them the address of the cottage. If indeed she was making for the cottage, it was going to need careful handling. The last thing she wanted was for a local bobby from Fort William turning up at the cottage unannounced. Cookson may panic and run again, taking the boy with her and they would be back to square one.

The news about the sighting on the motorway did indicate that they may be on the right track, but they needed more information before acting on it. Just because she was heading north didn't necessarily mean she was going to the Scottish Highlands. There were plenty of other possible destinations along the way.

Pete handed Alex a list of Cookson's previous addresses, all of which were in the Dorset area. He hadn't been able to find out much else. There was nothing on social media, not even Facebook or Twitter pages, not really surprising, as she would have been careful to keep a low profile. He had contacted her bank and credit card companies, at least the ones for which he had statements, and it appeared she hadn't used any of her cards or accounts so far. Of course, he said, she may have had other accounts and he would keep digging.

'Thanks Pete, that's great,' Alex said, then went on, 'Sally, I take it you've postponed the media appeal?'

'Yes Boss, but I had already contacted Ms Bolton and she had reluctantly agreed to do it. When I rang to tell her it had been postponed, in fact, she seemed rather relieved.'

'Did she? That's interesting,' Alex replied. 'We've still got surveillance on her haven't we?'

'Absolutely. If she makes a move, we'll be on it.'

'Well, it looks likely that Cookson has headed for

this cottage, or at least, to Scotland. If so, at some point I will have to make the decision whether we need to get ourselves up there. Neil, could you check up on the flights to Scotland. I'm not sure which airport would be nearest to Fort William, but we need to make contingency plans in case we need to go.'

'Sure thing, Boss, I'll get onto it straightaway.'

'Have you decided about the Child Rescue Alert yet Boss?' Sally asked.

'Well, I think we'll hold off just a little longer. If we're sure she's heading for the cottage, I think it would be best not to spook her by putting out a general alert.'

'Well, it's your call Boss,'

'I feel a 'but' coming on Sally. Spit it out.'

'Well,' Sally went on, 'it seems we're pinning everything on this cottage, when really we have no idea whether we're right about that.'

'I know, it is a fine judgement, but I think I understand how she must be feeling. At the moment, it's all about flight, but sooner or later she's going to begin to realise she's heading into a cul-de-sac, with no way out. I don't want to magnify that feeling. The longer she can believe they have escaped, the more time we will have to catch up with her before desperation drives her to do something stupid.'

'I see. You're probably right Boss.'

'As well as that, when she does begin to realise what a hopeless position she's in, I'm still hoping that she will contact Bolton to ask her to help her, and she will lead us directly to her. So, I just feel that we need to give it another few hours before instigating a CRA.'

'OK Boss.' Sally acceded.

'Boss!' Neil called across from his desk, 'The nearest airport to Fort William is Inverness, which is about seventy miles to the north. There's a flight from Bristol to Inverness at 10.35 tomorrow morning that gets in at 12.05.'

'Thanks Neil,' Alex acknowledged, 'Sally, could you book two seats on that flight and organise a hire car for when we arrive. Then can you establish contact with Fort William police to let them know we're coming and ask them if they could spare a local officer to assist us. Could you also check whether they have had any sightings of the car.'

***

With that, Alex retired to her office to think through the events of the day. In her own mind she was pretty certain that Cookson was on her way to Scotland, but she knew that until she had more proof, she had to keep an open mind. One of the dangers in this job was becoming too focussed on one particular possibility, which could close off consideration of other options.

All she knew with any certainty was that Cookson had taken the boy and left the house at 10 am on Monday. There had been a possible sighting of them on the M4 heading west, and a confirmed one on the M6 heading north. She also knew that as a child,

Cookson had spent family holidays at the cottage near Fort William, but she had to admit that was a fairly tenuous connection. Scotland was a sizeable country with relatively few roads and over seventy thousand square miles, much of it wild. She realised that her best bet would still be to follow Bolton, if she made a move. In the meantime, maybe the Fort William police would pick up the car, which would narrow down the options considerably.

***

Sally knocked on the door and came in with a piece of paper in her hand. Handing it to Alex, she began,

'OK Boss, you're booked on the flight to Inverness tomorrow. You need to be at the airport by nine. Who will you be taking with you?'

'I'll take Neil. Can you ask him to pick me up at home at eight? And tell him he needs to bring an overnight bag with stuff for a few days. Of course, this might change if we get more info in overnight. I want you to keep an eye on things this end Sally. We still need to be open to other possibilities. I want Pete to continue trying to pin down the owners of the cottage to find out if they are there. Let me know straight away if he has any success. I'll liaise with you about the CRA depending how things work out in the next day or two. What about a hire car by the way? We'll have a couple of hours drive to get down to Fort William.'

'That's all booked for you, it should be at the airport when you arrive. I've booked it as an open booking.

We just need to let them know when you're ready to hand it back.'

'Okay, well, I think that's about it for today. Let me know immediately day or night, if Bolton makes a move.'

'I will Boss, the surveillance team will follow her and contact me immediately if she does, and I will alert traffic to keep lookout for the car as well. I think we can be fairly certain she would have headed north, so hopefully, there will have been other sightings on the motorways.'

'That's fine. Well, I'll be in touch in the morning, and we'll make a final decision about Inverness.'

***

With that, Alex wrapped things up for the day and headed home. She would have to tell Dave she may be away for a few days from tomorrow, which he wouldn't be best pleased about. It would mean he would have to deal with the school runs and netball and cricket practice sessions as well as mealtimes. Still, she thought, he had known what he was taking on, marrying a policewoman! She supposed it didn't make it any easier though. He had his own job to hold down as well.

When she arrived at the house she found Dave and the kids eating dinner.

'We waited as long as we could love, but we were all feeling faint from lack of food!'

'Oh, I'm sorry, it's been a hell of a day, and worse

is to come I'm afraid. Tomorrow I may be off to Inverness and could be away for a couple of days.'

'So you won't be here on Saturday! But mum. I thought you were going to come along to watch me play. It's the junior league championship! You promised!'

'I know love, and I'm sorry Johnny, but if I get the news I'm expecting later, this is something I can't get out of. It's a serious case and time critical, so I have no choice I'm afraid.'

At that, Johnny, who had just finished eating, stomped off up to his room, slamming his bedroom door.

It was about ten o'clock that Sally rang to say she'd just had a call from Fort William police. Cookson and Archie had been picked up on a camera heading north out of Glasgow, toward Loch Lomond. Now Alex was sure that she was indeed heading towards Fort William, and told Sally to give Neil a ring to let him know that their trip to Scotland for tomorrow was definitely on.

'Will do Boss,' Sally replied, 'speak tomorrow.'

Alex's head was buzzing now. It looked like she'd been right.

'Well that's it love, I'm definitely heading up to Scotland in the morning,' she told Dave, who was looking at her questioningly, having heard the mention of a trip.

'Any idea how long you'll be away?'

'Not sure, hopefully no more than a couple of days if all goes well.'

OK, no problem,' he replied, 'just keep in touch. I still worry about you, you know.'

'I know you do love, but, really there's no need, I don't take any unnecessary risks you know, with you and the kids waiting for me back here.'

Chapter Twenty-Two

As she was waiting for Neil to collect her the next morning, she rang Dorothy and Ted. She usually called them on Saturday morning. As she would be travelling most of the day and tied up with goodness knows what, she felt this would be a good time to ring. Ted picked up the phone.

'Hello love, it's good to hear from you, but you're a bit early, mum's still in bed.'

'Hello Dad. Yes, I'm sorry but I have to go out on a case soon, so I thought I'd ring you before I left. Is mum ok? She's usually up by now.'

'Well, she's been a bit tired lately love, so I've persuaded her to take things a bit easier, and she's taken to lying in a little later these days.'

'When's her next check up Dad?'

'In a couple of weeks I think. But try not to worry, I'm sure it's nothing serious. After all, we're not getting any younger and we can't expect to do what we used to do, can we?'

'Well, I have to go up to Scotland on a job for a couple of days, and I'm being picked up any minute, so tell her to take it easy and I'll ring her when I get back.'

'OK love, and you take care now, whatever this job is.'

'Of course I will. Give Mum my love. Bye Dad.'

***

Neil turned up at eight o'clock sharp, and Alex was ready and waiting. Shouting her goodbyes to Dave and the kids, she stepped out of one life, as a wife and mother, slamming the door behind her, and into her other life, as 'Boss'.

The traffic wasn't too bad, and they arrived at Bristol airport in plenty of time. They parked up and headed into the terminal, picking up a coffee on the way to the check-in desk. An hour later they were in the air on their way to Scotland.

Sitting near the window, Alex watched the landscape far below gradually change from city to a patchwork of fields, more cities, then the hills of the Lake District with its lakes looking like tiny mirrors glinting in the sunlight. Finally, after more fields and meadows, they passed over Glasgow and after that the landscape soon changed once again as the hills and lochs of the Highlands came into view. Even at this height it was breath-taking, quite unlike any of the other landscapes they had flown over on the journey.

The flight touched down at Inverness airport at precisely one o'clock, and as Alex and Neil left the airport building, a rep from the car hire firm was waiting for them. Alex showed him her ID card and he handed over the keys, saying that it had half a tank of petrol, but there was a station a mile or so down the road, so if they were going any distance, they ought to fill up, as there weren't too many garages in the Highlands. She signed the paperwork he'd produced and thanked him, before throwing the keys to Neil and settling into the passenger seat.

Alex set the satnav on her phone to Fort William police station as Neil was filling up the tank. They picked up sandwiches and a couple of cans and then set off down the road. Alex rang the office for an update.

'Hi Sally, are Fort William aware we'll be with them shortly?

'Yes, they are. A DS Campbell is waiting for you there.'

'Good. Has Pete had any joy about the cottage?'

'He has, I'll text you the full address. However, he still can't locate the owner to find out if Cookson is there, so I guess you'll just have to go and check it out.'

'OK Sally, we'll certainly do that. If she isn't there, we're going to look pretty stupid though, and worryingly, it may turn out that I've got it all wrong and she's somewhere else entirely. I'll be in touch later.'

'Ok Boss, we'll speak later then.'

'OK, well once we've collected DS Campbell, we'll head over to the cottage.

'OK Boss, bye for now.'

As they drove along, having an hour or so before

they would arrive at Fort William, Alex allowed herself to relax a little and enjoy the scenery.

'Have you been to Scotland before Neil?'

'No Boss, I haven't, but it's pretty impressive, isn't it?' he replied.

'It certainly is. A bit wild in places for my taste though, to be honest.'

They each sank into their own thoughts for a while, then Neil asked her,

'Do you have any thoughts about how we're going to handle this Boss? It strikes me that Cookson is going to be feeling pretty desperate.'

'She is Neil, and we are going to have to tread carefully.'

'OK Boss,' he replied, as the satnav told him that they were reaching their destination, and he pulled into the carpark of Fort William police station.

***

Archie had been skimming stones across the surface of the loch. Right now, he felt happy. He'd enjoyed the journey with his mum, and they'd spent the last three days exploring the area. She'd been telling him stories about the people who used to live here. Exciting stories about battles between what they called 'clans'. She'd even bought him a book at the place in Glencoe, which he'd already started to read.

However, he still couldn't quite understand why they had come away so suddenly and travelled so far. It wasn't the school holidays, and his mum was usually very keen that he shouldn't miss even a day of school. Then there was the phone. why hadn't she used it since they left home. He hadn't seen her ring Sam once. Had they fallen out? Was that it? Was she hiding from her? But that didn't make sense. His mum was the one who was renting the house they lived in. Surely if they had fallen out, Sam would have been the one to leave? Then another thought struck him. Was it something to do with Jack? She had behaved very strangely after we left the boatyard, he thought. Surely, she hadn't done all this to keep him away from Jack and Ben?

He decided he would have to ask her to explain what was going on, and after they had eaten lunch, he tentatively broached the subject.

'Mum,' he said.

'Yes love?' she answered.

'It's really great to be here with you.'

'That's nice dear, I'm glad you're enjoying it.'

'I am, but mum, I am a bit confused.'

Alice looked a little uncomfortable, saying, 'Why love, what's the matter?'

'Well,' Archie went on, 'I'm not really sure why we're here. I should be in school really, shouldn't I? So how long are we staying? Did Sam know we were leaving? Does she know where we are?'

In full swing now, and against his better judgement, but unable to stop himself, he continued, 'You've never used your phone once since we left home and she's never rung. Have you fallen out? I hope not, I like Sam really. I'm sorry I shouted at her about not being able to stop me seeing Jack. Is all this my fault mum?'

Alice held out her arms saying, 'Come here love,' before giving him a hug.

'Look, I just thought we needed to be on our own for a while. I think I may have been neglecting you for some time, what with being involved with Sam, but you are still my number one priority Archie, and I wanted you to know that. Do you understand?'

Basking in the warmth of her embrace and loving words, Archie felt reassured and decided he didn't need to know why they were here, but just to enjoy spending this time with her.

***

In Fort William, Alex and Neil got out of the car and entered the police station. A young detective was in the reception area, obviously waiting for them. Alex offered him her hand, saying,

'DS Campbell, I suppose?'

'Yes ma'am, Charlie Campbell,' he replied.

'Good to meet you DS Campbell,' she said, 'I'm DI Alex Scott and this is DC Neil Cotton.'

'We need to move fast Charlie, have they filled you in as to what's going on?'

'I've had a short briefing Ma'am, but perhaps you can fill in the details as we are travelling.'

'Have your CCTV cameras come up with anything? '

'Yes Ma'am, we contacted the Glencoe visitor centre, as anyone heading this way from Glasgow would most likely pass that way, and we had some luck.

They checked their cameras in the shop and from the photos we had sent, they identified them as having visited the shop on Tuesday afternoon.'

'That's great news, so it confirms that more than likely they were on their way here.'

'It looks that way, but alternatively they could have taken the Corran Ferry towards Strontian.' Charlie Campbell postulated.

'Right, well, we'll soon find out if we're right about this cottage, so let's go and find out, shall we?' Alex replied.'

As they were driving the ten miles or so to the cottage, Alex gave him a quick rundown of the events of the past few days.

'So, as of now, we think we know where she's staying,' showing him the address on her phone. 'We'll need to exercise caution though, and maybe park some way off and approach on foot.'

'Seems like a plan, Ma'am,' he agreed.

Fifteen minutes later they were driving along the side of the loch, when in the distance they could see a turn off to the right. Checking the satnav Alex could see that this lane would lead to the cottage a quarter of a mile or so from the main road.

'OK Neil, take this next turn on the right. The cottage is about a quarter of a mile down the lane but pull in a couple of hundred yards or so from it and we'll walk the rest of the way.'

'OK Boss,' he affirmed.

After he'd turned off the main road into the lane he

pulled up in front of a field gate a couple of hundred yards along. The three of them walked along the side of the road, making sure that they were out of the line of sight of anyone in the cottage. As they approached, they could see that there was no car parked anywhere in the vicinity.

'There's no car Ma'am,' Charlie Campbell stated.

'Maybe they've gone off somewhere,' Alex replied.

They were peering from behind the stone wall to one side of the property.

'Let's move in cautiously to take a closer look.'

However, as they drew nearer, Alex began to feel a little apprehensive. The place looked completely deserted. There were no curtains at the window, and the place had an air of neglect about it.

'It's not looking good is it Ma'am?' Charlie said.

'No, it looks deserted,' Alex replied, 'but I guess it's possible she's still staying here though. She may be squatting.'

'That's true, but they're obviously not here at the moment. Shall I take a look through the window?'

'Yes, go ahead, but be careful. We can't risk spooking her, or the boy, and remember, he does have his dog with him,' Alex told him.

Campbell crouched down and ran quickly to the corner of the cottage, then inched his way along to the window. He peered in and then quickly stood up, beckoning Alex and Neil to follow him.

As they approached, he called out,

'There's definitely no-one staying here Ma'am. It's completely empty.'

Alex joined him at the window and told Neil to check around the back in case there were any signs of life there. Neil returned in less than a minute

'No sign of life Boss, doesn't look like anyone's stayed here in years.'

Alex was devastated. She had been so sure Cookson would be here. Now what?

'OK, nothing to be done here, we need to rethink this one. Let's get back to the station.'

As they drove along, Alex rang Sally to let her know that they had drawn a blank at the cottage.

'It does seem though, that they did pass through Glencoe on Tuesday afternoon. They were spotted on their CCTV. So, they must have been heading this way. No movement from Sam Bolton, I suppose?'

'No Boss, nothing yet.' Sally replied. 'Are you ready to alert the CRA yet?'

'Not quite Sally, let's give it another twenty-four hours. Neil and I will book into an hotel here for tonight. Maybe the local force will have some more information or sightings by then and we can decide what to do next.'

'OK Boss, I'll let you know if anything happens this end.'

'Thanks Sally,' Alex signed off as they drove into the carpark of the Police Station.

Chapter Twenty-Three

That night, as she tried to sleep, Alice was wondering what on earth she should do next. So far, her only thoughts had been about getting as far away from Long and the police as possible. However, after her conversation with Archie earlier, the reality of her situation struck her like a thunderbolt. What on earth was she doing? Panic began to rise in her throat as she lay there. How long would it be before they tracked her down? She knew there were many ways they might do that. She felt she had been careful and had probably bought herself some time, but what then? She couldn't take Archie abroad without a passport. She thought about Sam. Would she, could she, help her? She had no one else to turn to. Maybe she should have trusted her from the start. Was it now too late to ask her? What else could she do?

For hours she wrestled with her thoughts, trying desperately to decide what to do. She hardly slept. It was going round and round in her head. She couldn't stay here forever and yet she couldn't go back. She would never give Archie up. He was hers. She'd given up her child once, but never again. Finally at two o'clock in the morning, in desperation she decided she had to ask Sam for help and would send her a WhatsApp message. She daren't risk a text in case the police were monitoring her phone calls. It would be a bit of a risk even switching it on, but she had no other way to get in touch with her. She got out of bed and retrieved her phone from the bottom of her bag.

With a deep breath she opened WhatsApp and quickly typed the address and postcode for the cottage with the words, 'I need your help! Please don't tell the police. Please come, I love you.' She hesitated with her finger over the 'send' button. Did she love her enough to help her? She felt sure now that she did. She had said she loved her more than she had ever loved anyone else, and she had been convinced Sam was going to propose that night – the night everything changed. So, after a brief hesitation, she pressed the button. She was sure Sam would respond as soon as she got the message, and she waited expectantly.

***

Sam was in a light sleep when she heard the phone ping on the table beside her. She knew from the tone it was a WhatsApp message and she knew the only person who would be messaging in the middle of the night would be Alice. She grabbed the phone and opened up the page. It was as she had expected, from Alice. She was asking her to go to her and had given her the address. She was in Scotland! Everything was ready. The car was topped up and her bags packed. All she needed to do was to get in the car and drive.

Yet something was stopping her. She thought about what Alice had done. How could she not? What she had done to Archie and his family all those years ago was unforgiveable, resulting in the death of his mother, and depriving Archie of the love of his own family. And Jack! He had suffered the loss of his family and the life they had shared. He had been forced into a solitary existence. Much as she loved the Alice she had known, when it came to it, Sam couldn't forgive or forget what she'd done. She thought about replying to her but realised that if Alice was sure she wasn't coming, she may panic and run again. It would be better not to reply at all, but to let the police know where she was. It broke her heart to let Alice down like this, but what else could she do? The boy must be brought back and returned to his father and Alice must face the consequences of what she'd done. She would be desperate, she knew that, but she also felt that the safest way for this to end would be for the police to handle it, and so she didn't send a reply.

***

Alice waited and waited for her answer, but it never came and after an hour she gave up and turned off her phone. So that was it, she was on her own and she had badly misjudged Sam's reaction. She should never have given her the address, at least until she had said she was coming to her. Would she betray her to the police? Well, as Sam had made her choice not to help her, she must be prepared for that too.

They were going to have to move on again. Taking out the atlas she tried to find an escape route. Not that easy, she thought, in the Highlands. Roads are few with hardly any roads leading off them. In the end she decided their best plan was to avoid travelling back through Glencoe and Glasgow. She knew there were ferries from Campbeltown. Turning on her phone she quickly found out that there was one going to Ardrossan. From there she could drive south to Cairnryan and catch the ferry to Larne or Belfast. From there she could drive down to the south. Maybe they could lose themselves there. So this was the plan she settled on. Unfortunately, it would still involve driving back to the Corran Ferry, after which she could leave the road to Glencoe and head south to Campbeltown. It was a five-hour drive but it would mean she could miss Glasgow out completely.

By now it was four am. She must get some sleep; she had a long drive ahead of her. She knew that if Sam did give the address to the police, she wouldn't have long to get away, but felt she could be across the ferry and on her way to Campbeltown before they turned up.

***

After a few hours' sleep she was woken by Archie crashing in with Trixie, saying they were going for a walk down to the loch.

'OK, don't be long, and no swimming! I think we'll move on today.'

'Move on! Where to?'

'Not sure yet love, it'll be a surprise for us both,' she replied, as brightly as she could manage. 'Anyway, you can nip down to the water while I pack up but be back in an hour. As soon as we've had some breakfast, we'll be on our way.'

'But I like it here mum,' Archie sighed, 'I don't understand why we have to keep moving. Are we running away or something?'

'Of course not love! Whatever made you think that? Go on, off you go now, and I'll have your breakfast ready when you get back.'

Archie and Trixie ran off to the water's edge to play a last game of skimming. Trixie wanted to go for a swim but Archie stopped her, mum wouldn't want a wet dog in the car, he thought. He was wondering why she had decided to move on. He liked it here, by the loch. But then, he still didn't really know why they were here at all!

Alice quickly washed and dressed, then packed up their things and slung the bags in the boot. She took out the atlas and memorised the route they must take to Campbeltown. Obviously, they would have to take the Corran Ferry across Loch Linnhe, but she couldn't avoid that, and just hoped that the police weren't already on the lookout for them.

When they had eaten breakfast, Alice told Archie to check that nothing had been left behind in his room, then to take Trixie for a last walk before putting her in the car. By ten o'clock, Alice was locking up the cottage and replacing the key under the stone where they had found it when they arrived.

Chapter Twenty-Four

Alex had rung Sally at nine o'clock and was pleased to hear that she'd just taken a call from Sam Bolton. Cookson had been in touch with him, via WhatsApp as they had expected, during the night, asking her to follow her. However, she'd decided she couldn't do that. Ms Bolton had realised that what Cookson had done was very wrong and wanted no part in it, but she knew that the boy should be returned to his father, and that Alice Cookson needed to face the consequences of what she'd done. Sam had given her the address Cookson had given her.

'Oh, don't tell me it's on the other side of Scotland!' Alex said.

'No, fortunately it's not too far from Fort William. It's down on Loch Sunart, but you'll need to take the Corran Ferry, which is about a half hour drive south from Fort William.'

'Brilliant Sally! So we now know exactly where they are. Does Cookson know she's not coming?'

'Well, I imagine so, because she didn't reply to her message.'

'Well, if she was foolish enough to give him the address, and if she thinks Bolton's not coming, she must suspect she will pass it on to us.'

'I guess so, Boss.'

Alice rang Charlie Campbell to tell him they needed to head down to Loch Sunart and to ask him if he could accompany them. He readily agreed and said he would be ready to be picked up from the station anytime. Alice sent Neil to collect him while she settled up with the hotel. In half an hour they arrived at the ferry terminal, and by ten o'clock were driving along the road to Loch Sunart.

***

Driving in the opposite direction was Alice Cookson. Neil, who was concentrating on the road ahead, saw her first, in the distance.

'Boss!' he exclaimed, 'That looks like a red Escort, coming towards us! It could be Cookson.'

'Slow down!' Alex told him, 'Let's take a look as they pass, and be ready to turn round to follow them.'

As the red car approached, Charlie said that it was definitely a Ford Escort, and as it drove past, Alex could see that a blond woman was driving, and a smaller person was sitting in the passenger seat. The clincher though, was the blond Labrador with its head half poking out of the open window in the back. As it drove away from them Alex checked the number, confirming that it was indeed Alice Cookson.

'It's them!' Alex declared, 'Come on, let's go!'

Neil quickly carried out a three-point turn and set off in pursuit.

Alice had noticed the black car moving slowly along towards them and in the rear-view mirror could see that it had turned round and was now driving along the road behind her. Her stomach churned. Could it be the police? Had Sam told them where she was? How could she betray her like that?

She speeded up, her foot down hard on the accelerator pedal. If the car speeded up too, she would know. It did. Oh God she thought, what the hell am I going to do now? Archie wanted to know why she was going so fast, but she didn't answer him, her attention on the car behind, which was now obviously trying to keep up with her. With a shock she realised that they would be bound to catch up with her at the ferry. She knew she was driving too fast for the conditions of the road, but she had to shake them off somehow. She wouldn't let anyone take Archie away.

She remembered there was a right turn somewhere along the road before it veered to the left and up towards Corran. The road had dipped slightly and looking ahead she could see the turn off at the top of the rise. She had no idea where it led to but at least she could keep driving and hope that somehow, she could give the car behind the slip at some point. Carrying on to the ferry would certainly mean that they would catch up with her.

By now Archie was afraid. He knew his mum was driving too fast.

'Slow down mum!' he cried.

She didn't answer him but suddenly slowed the car, causing Trixie to fall backwards and then across the back seat with a squeal, as she threw the car round the corner into the road going off to the right. The car behind followed and now she knew for sure. It must be the police.

'Mum! What are you doing? Slow down! You've hurt Trixie!'

Alex was concerned that Cookson was obviously driving too fast.

'OK Neil, she's realised that we're following her, and I don't want to push her too hard, so stay back a bit. Where does this road lead Charlie?'

'It just follows the edge of the loch down to Kilmalieu Ma'am, but it's not the easiest road for anyone who is unfamiliar with it, with several hairpins. It also runs very close to the water in several places. Not the best place for a high-speed chase.'

***

Alice checked the mirror. The car behind had slowed slightly. Maybe now if she put her foot down, she could leave them behind, or get far enough ahead that she could turn off this road without them seeing where she'd gone. She stamped on the accelerator and the car lurched forward at top speed. Somewhere in the distance she could hear Archie shouting to her to stop, but her mind wasn't functioning now, apart from telling her to escape. She had to. She wouldn't give up her child. He was hers. He had been hers from the moment she'd set eyes on him. They had taken him away from her once, they weren't going to do it again.

The car squealed round two hairpin bends, but the third proved too much. Archie screamed. Alice froze as they left the road and headed for the loch. The shore was rocky, and the car flipped then rolled then flipped again until it reached the water, where, now the right way up, it slowly began to sink. Alice had sustained a bump on the head as the roof of the car had collapsed slightly on the driver's side and was only half conscious.

'Mum! Mum!' Archie screamed, 'we've got to get out!'

Survival instinct kicked in and he managed to open his door and climb out before the car filled up with water. He remembered Trixie and swam under the water to open the back door of the car when she swam out and followed him up to the surface.

The shock of the cold water on her face brought Alice back to full consciousness and she tried to open her door to follow Archie. With rising terror, she realised it was stuck. The frame must have distorted when the car rolled, and it wouldn't budge.

Neil, Alex and Charlie had been a hundred yards or so behind the Escort and had watched in horror as it left the road. When they arrived at the scene, Neil had jumped out of the car and run to the water's edge. He could see the boy and the dog swimming towards the shore but there was no sign of the woman. He entered the water and started swimming towards Archie, who shouted to him that his mum was still in the car. Alex was now standing at the water's edge and waded in to help the boy to safety. He was screaming that his mum was still in the car.

By now, Neil had dived down towards the car, which was still sinking. He managed to reach it and could see the woman was still sitting in the driver's seat. He tried to open the door, but it was stuck fast. She was struggling to open it and he motioned to her to move over to the passenger side, where the door was still open. He returned to the surface to take a breath then dived back down on the other side of the car. Alice was struggling to move across to the passenger seat. Neil could see that in her confusion she hadn't yet released the seatbelt, so he reached into the car to free her. She was desperately trying to hold on to what breath she had left, but with the extra effort of trying to move across to climb out of the door, she finally lost the fight. Suddenly she stopped struggling and it was obvious to Neil he had to get her out of the water quickly. He grabbed her under her arms and pulled her clear of the car just as it suddenly settled further under the water.

Archie was crying out over and over that they had to get his mum out. He tried to pull away from Alex to go back in the water to save her, but she held him tight, telling him that it would be alright, they would get her out. Trixie was barking, sensing the panic in

Archie's voice. After what seemed like an eternity, Neil finally surfaced and swam towards the shore supporting Alice, who looked unconscious.

Meanwhile, Charlie had been on the phone to the ambulance service and told Alex they were on their way. Neil had dragged the apparently lifeless Alice clear of the water, then he and Charlie carried her up on to the flat surface of the road and laid her on her back on Charlie's coat. Archie was distraught, crying out to his mother to wake up. Alex held him back while Charlie began to administer mouth to mouth, and Neil worked on her chest to maintain some blood flow through her heart.

'What are they doing?' Archie screamed. But he'd seen enough television dramas to know what this meant, and he shouted out, 'Mum! Wake up! Don't leave me!' Although it was the last thing Archie wanted to do, Alex knew she had to persuade him to get out of his wet clothes. She found some dry things from Neil's luggage and helped Archie to get into them.

Seemingly endless minutes ticked by with no sign of the ambulance. After what he'd just been through and with the effort of trying to keep Alice alive, Neil was almost exhausted, and very cold. They were on the point of giving up, when in the distance, they heard the siren of the ambulance.

Relieved, Charlie and Neil stood back to allow the paramedics to do their work. They quickly transferred Alice to the ambulance and started to work on her once again. After another ten minutes they tried using a defibrillator and after a couple of tries they detected a faint pulse. Once they were confident she was stable enough, they told Alex they would be taking her up to Belford Hospital in Fort William, and Alex said they would follow, along with the boy. The paramedics also insisted that Neil get checked over. He was shaking now, obviously in the first stages of hypothermia. He clambered into the ambulance and they threw a blanket around him.

***

Archie wanted to go with his mum, but Alex persuaded him they would need to get Trixie into the car and might need his help to do that. He realised she was right. Trixie would need him. She wouldn't want to go with strangers. Alex promised she would take him to his mum at the hospital. The ambulance sped away towards the Corran Ferry, and Charlie turned the car around, then got out and opened the doors for Archie and Trixie to climb into the back seat.

'Take us straight to the hospital Charlie. When we get there we'll have to ask you to take care of the dog while we go in to see how things are.'

'Trixie!' Archie called out from the back seat. 'She's called Trixie!'

'Yes, of course. Trixie. I'm sorry Archie, I didn't know her name.' Alex apologised.

Alex rang Sally to let her know what had happened and that they were on their way to the hospital. She asked her to contact Fort William to ask them if they could arrange for someone to meet them there, to take care of Archie. Charlie will deal with Archie's dog, Trixie, she told her.

'OK Boss, I'll get onto it right away. Is Neil alright?'

'Well, he's gone in the ambulance. He was a bit hypothermic, understandably, but I'm sure he'll be fine,' Alex assured her.

Chapter Twenty-Five

Sam was feeling guilty. She had betrayed the woman she loved. She was afraid what the consequences might be. If the police didn't handle things well, goodness knows what might happen. It was Saturday and with no work to take her mind off things, her imagination was running riot. She felt she wanted to speak to Jack Long. She needed to reassure herself that she'd done the right thing.

Finally, she jumped in the car and drove to the canal carpark. She soon found the Lady Louise. Jack was sitting on top of the boat, painting, as usual. Ben jumped down and barked a greeting.

'Hello,' Jack said, 'Have you heard anything?'

'Can I come aboard? I need to talk to you,' Sam replied.

'Sure,' Jack agreed, 'I was just going to have a brew, would you like one?'

'Thanks,' Sam answered as she walked across the gangplank and jumped down into the cockpit.

As they sat down with their tea, Jack asked Sam what news she had for him. Sam didn't really know where to start because she still wasn't sure she'd done the right thing. Had telling the police where they were made things safer for Archie, or caused him to be put in danger? So much depended on things outside his control. How would the police handle it?

Finally, he began, 'I had a message from Alice in the night, telling me where they are and asking me to go to them.'

'What?! Where are they?'

'In Scotland,' Sam went on. 'She wanted me to go to her, but I couldn't do it. Even though I love her, I know what she did was wrong. Archie belongs with you and Alice will have to face the consequences.'

Jack sat back in amazement. Like the police, he had assumed that if Cookson contacted Sam for help, she would go to her. It seemed he had misjudged her.

'What are you going to do about it then?'

'I've already done it,' Sam replied. 'I've already told the police and given them the address, but now, I'm terrified that I've done the wrong thing. If they don't handle it carefully, it may just make matters worse.'

'Well, I don't see what else you could have done. Even if you had decided to go to her, you would undoubtedly have led them to her in any case.'

'I guess that's true, I know they've been watching me. Anyway, I thought you should know, in case the police hadn't told you that they now know where they are.'

'Well, I'm grateful that you have. At least now there's a chance that Toby will be brought back. I've been out of my mind, as you can imagine, and feeling utterly helpless. I really do appreciate what you've done. I'll ring the police now to see what they're doing about finding them.'

With that, Jack phoned the station, asking to speak to DI Alex Scott. The call was put through to Sally.

'DS Nugent, can I help you?' Sally began.

'Hello, it's Jack Long here. Ms Bolton has just told me that you now have an address where Ms Cookson is staying with my son. I'm just ringing to see if there have been any developments.'

'Good morning, Mr Long. Well, DCI Scott travelled to Scotland yesterday as we had some intelligence that suggested she was heading that way. When Ms Bolton gave us the address DCI Scott and DC Cotton were able to intercept Ms Cookson.'

'You mean you've got her in custody? What about my son.'

'He's safe and well and with DCI Scott. I'm afraid there was an accident though. Ms Cookson was driving too fast and the car left the road, plunging into the water. Archie swam clear with his dog but I'm afraid Ms Cookson wasn't so lucky. Although DC Cotton helped her to escape, she is still unconscious.'

Jack looked at Sam, who had been able to hear what DS Nugent had been saying. The colour had drained from her face. She snatched the phone from Jack and shouted into it,

'Is Alice alright?! Where is she now?!'

'Who is this?' Sally asked.

'It's Sam Bolton here. I came to tell Jack – Mr Long that I had heard from her. But tell me what's happened – is Alice alright?'

'Well, I believe it was touch and go for a while, but they managed to stabilise her and she's now in hospital in Fort William.'

'For God's sake, look after her. She's going to be distraught. Now she will be aware she's going to lose Archie. She could do anything!'

'We are aware of that Ms Bolton, and we are of course keeping a close eye on her.'

Jack could stand it no longer and snatched the phone back, demanding to know about Toby.

'Where is my son? Is he alright? What's going to happen next?'

Sally reassured him once again that he was safe and DCI Scott was taking care of him. Beyond that, she couldn't say what would happen next, but would be speaking to DCI Scott later and would let him know what had been decided. The lad would obviously want to stay near to Ms Cookson for the moment, but it was possible she would be transferred to a hospital in the area when it was safe to do so, and of course, Archie would then be brought back with her.

***

After an hour or so in the warmth of the hospital and with a couple of hot drinks inside him, Neil had recovered from his ordeal.

'That was a brave thing you did Neil,' his boss told him. 'You saved a life today.'

'Just instinctive Boss, anyone would have done the same.'

'Not 'anyone' Neil,' Alex replied with a smile.

She looked across at Archie, who was sitting in the waiting room with Brenda Taylor, a social worker Fort William had sent along to take charge of him for the moment. He looked lost and rather neglected, wearing Neil's jumper and shorts which of course were far too big for him. She went over to him and said,

'The doctor says you can see your mum soon, Archie.'

Chapter Twenty-Six

It was half an hour later that Alex and Neil heard the alarm going off in Cookson's cubicle. Staff were dashing from all directions.

'Oh my God,' Alex said quietly to Neil, and then looked across at Archie, who obviously also knew what that meant. He jumped up and started to run towards the cubicle, but Alex intercepted him, saying,

'Archie, let the doctors do their work.'

'I want to see my mum!' he retorted, 'I'm not stupid you know, I know she already died once! Let me go!' he shouted, 'I want to see her!'

Still Alex held him fast. Over the next few minutes there was frantic activity behind the curtain. Then they heard,

'Stand clear!' followed by the unmistakeable thump of a defibrillator, and there was no doubt as to what was going on behind that curtain.

Twice more they tried to restart her heart but eventually they heard,

'Everyone ready to call it?' followed by assenting noises, then the statement,

'Life extinct at 12.45 pm'

Archie screamed

'Nooo! Mum! Don't leave me!' then he finally tore himself from Alex's grip and ran to the cubicle.

He threw himself onto his mother, repeating, 'No! No! No! Mum, don't leave me.'

One of the nurses gently put her arms round his shoulders saying,

'I'm so sorry,' at which point Archie shrugged her arms away screaming,

'You could have saved her! Why didn't you save her! She was alive when she came in here. What have you done to her!' Then he ran from the cubicle and straight into Alex's arms.

Alex held on to him as he broke down sobbing, then after a minute or two he suddenly stiffened and pulled away from her, shouting,

'You've all killed my mum! If you hadn't chased us she'd still be alive now!'

Alex's mind was working overtime. How on earth would she handle this now? The child had just lost his mother. He was angry, of course, and he would want answers. Why was his mother running away? What had she done that was so wrong? He would want to know, but how could she tell him that his mother wasn't his mother, that she had stolen him from his real mother? She felt completely out of her depth and realised she would need to get him back home and find some help to deal with this if the boy wasn't to be permanently damaged by the truths he would inevitably have to be told.

Alex shot a pleading look at Brenda Taylor, who immediately recognised that her input was needed and quickly strode over to Archie to offer him some comfort. After his initial outbursts he seemed more receptive to her approach, and she put her arms round him to comfort him. He was crying but silently now and looked utterly bewildered. He couldn't understand how life could change so much in a single moment.

***

Alex told Brenda that she needed to make a phone call and went outside to call Sally. She was shocked of course, to hear the news.

'Oh no! What about the boy?' she asked.

'Well, I think the priority will be to get him back home. Can you book another seat on a flight later today, some time after six. I've got one or two loose ends to tie up here first. I'm hoping to arrange for the body to be transferred. There'll have to be a PM and an inquest, but I'm counting on that being able to be done back there. The lad will have to be told everything eventually, of course, but we're going to need help with that. Can you get on to Social Services and explain the situation. Tell them we need a Social Worker with the right skills to be allocated to him immediately. Depending what they say I guess initially he could probably return to the family home with Sam Bolton, but obviously Jack Long will be making a claim on him. Poor lad, what a mess!'

'It surely is, Boss. I'll text you details of the ticket, shall I?'

'Yes, do that Sally. I'll ring you as soon as we land at Bristol, to see what arrangements Social Services have made.'

'What about his dog?'

'Oh God, yes, I'd almost forgotten about that. He's going to need his dog. I'll arrange for the RSPCA to transfer her.'

'OK Boss, see you later. Bye for now.'

Alex then rang the Fort William police station and asked to speak to DS Campbell. She was put straight through to his office. He was shocked when she gave him the news that Cookson had passed away.

'I'm hoping that I can get the body transferred down south, and intend taking the boy back later to-day, but I'm wondering if the RSPCA could take the dog home? We'll have to pay of course, but the lad is going to need his dog more than ever. He's going to have to deal with a lot more than the death of his mother, poor kid,' she went on.

'OK Ma'am, I'll get onto that and see what they suggest. The dog's here with me at the moment, in case he asks.'

As Alex went back into A&E, Neil approached her, looking distraught.

'I thought we'd saved her Boss. I should have been quicker!'

'Neil,' Alex said firmly, 'you did your best, you couldn't have done more.'

Neil didn't look as if he believed a word of it.

Alex walked slowly over to where Archie was sitting slumped against Brenda Taylor, who was holding him close. He looked utterly spent now, lost and so vulnerable it broke Alex's heart. She spoke to Brenda,

'I think we need to find somewhere ...'

'There's a relative's room I believe,' said Brenda, immediately understanding the unspoken question.

The receptionist had observed all the events of the last few minutes and, realising they needed some privacy walked over to them, inviting them to follow her to the relative's rest room down the corridor. Once they were in the room, Alex took charge of the situation as sensitively as she could. She explained to Archie that in a little while, if he wanted to see his mum again, that would be fine. Then later, she would take him back home. Trixie would be taken home by the RSPCA as she wouldn't be allowed on the plane.

Archie still looked bewildered, as though he didn't understand a word she was saying.

'Where am I going?' he asked finally. 'Who's going to look after me and Trixie now?'

'Don't worry, Archie, you'll be taken care of. We just need to get you both back home.'

'I can't leave mum here!' he suddenly shouted.

'No, of course not. Your mum will be taken home as soon as the police here will allow it.'

'I don't understand any of this,' Archie said suddenly. 'Why were you chasing us? This is all your fault.

If you hadn't been chasing us none of this would have happened!'

'I know your head must be full of questions Archie, and you will get all the answers, I promise, but first, we need to get home to Wiltshire.'

Just then a text popped up on Alex's phone. It was Sally with details of the flight she had booked Archie on. Their own tickets were open returns and there were plenty of seats available 7.30 pm flight.

Alex popped out of the room to speak to Neil. She asked him to go and buy some clothes for Archie, then rang DI Campbell again to ask him to pick them up from the hospital. She would need to speak to someone about arranging for the body to be sent down to Wiltshire. Also, she assumed the Scottish Police would probably want a statement from her before she left. Charlie Campbell confirmed that they certainly would, and he wasn't too sure whether the body would be released or whether they would insist on the PM being carried out in their own facility. He said he would arrange for her to see DSU Donald McDougall when they returned to the station, who would need to speak to the Crown Office and Procurator Fiscal Service before agreeing to the transfer. Alex thanked him and said they should be ready to leave in about half an hour.

Chapter Twenty-Seven

Neil had returned with some clothes for Archie, and when he had changed, Brenda had taken him in to see his mother one last time. All the tubes had been removed and she looked as though she was sleeping. Understandably, he was very upset and didn't want to leave her when the time came. Brenda reassured him that she would be sent down to Wiltshire and he would be able to see her again there if he wished. Reluctantly he had allowed himself to be led out of the room and to the waiting car. Once again, he had felt powerless to resist.

It was good to see Trixie at the station though; he had been worried about her. After all it had been an ordeal for her too! In the event, she didn't seem to have suffered any injuries and was delighted to see him. Charlie Campbell had arranged for Trixie to be collected from the station at three o'clock, so Archie was able to say goodbye to her before they set off to Inverness. He spent half an hour or so with her until the RSPCA man turned up to take her away. Archie was upset to be parted from her of course, but the

RSPCA man was very kind and assured him that Trixie would be with him by the afternoon of the following day.

At first DSU McDougall said that he didn't think the authorities would release the body as the death had occurred within their jurisdiction. However, Alex explained the circumstances, particularly around Archie's history. This wasn't only about a death of someone he had always known as his mother. It was also about returning the boy to his father, from whom he had been stolen ten years previously. After extensive discussion a compromise was reached. It was agreed that a post-mortem be carried out in Fort William, and Alex and Neil could submit their statements electronically, after they had been authenticated by a superior officer in Wiltshire. In any case their statements would no doubt be corroborated by Charlie Campbell's. Cookson's body would be released after the post-mortem and could then be forwarded to Wiltshire for the funeral.

***

Alex wasn't sure what she expected of Archie on the journey home. In fact he hardly spoke and she decided he was probably still in shock. He did however seem interested in the flight. He said he'd never been in a plane before and spent most of the journey staring out of the window at the landscape below.

When they landed, Alex rang Sally to ask what arrangements had been made for Archie. It appeared that he could spend the night in his own home, where a social worker called Mandy Williams would meet them. She would probably stay the night to ensure Archie was okay and tomorrow a decision would be made on the next steps to be taken. Alex was relieved. She had hoped he would be able to go home, for this evening at least. He would be better in familiar surroundings, and if they were to move him, he would be able to pick up some of his belongings.

The first Sam knew that Alice had passed away was when the social worker turned up on the doorstep. She was devastated. It was what she had been dreading all along. Of course, Mandy Williams didn't have any of the details about what had happened but said that DCI Scott was on her way from the airport with Archie, and would no doubt be able to tell him everything.

When Alex and Archie arrived at the house, Archie charged upstairs to his room and slammed his door shut. He was home, in his own space, and in spite of everything it felt good. When Sam saw Archie, she was consumed with guilt. She had caused the lad to lose his mother. If she hadn't given the address to the police ...

He questioned Alex intently, trying to understand exactly what had happened.

'I begged you to be careful, given her state of mind!' he almost shouted.

'Ms Bolton, we were careful. We stayed well back on that road, but she was determined to lose us and slammed her foot down on the accelerator. She was simply driving too fast for the road conditions and missed the corner. We did try to save her. DC Neil Cotton dived in without concern for himself and pulled her out of the sinking car. We carried out CPR and mouth to mouth at the scene until the paramedics arrived, and when they put her into the ambulance there was a faint pulse. However, in the end, her heart stopped, and they tried to revive her at the hospital, but, to no avail I'm afraid.'

Sam sat with her head in her hands, then asked,

'How much does Archie know?'

'Nothing at the moment, although his head is full of questions. However, we felt that should be left to the professionals.' Alex replied, glancing at Mandy Williams.

'Do we know what plans have been made for Archie yet?' she asked the social worker.

'Nothing definite as yet. As we all know, this is a very tricky situation that will need careful handling. Before we try to decide his future, he's going to need support to get through the next few weeks. We understand that it may be some time before the body is released for a funeral, which isn't going to help the process.'

'That's true. The PM is to be carried out in Scotland before the body is transferred. At that point they may give the go-ahead for the funeral, but alternatively they may decide to delay that until after the inquest, which may be several weeks away.'

'Well, let's hope, for Archie's sake, that doesn't

happen. As for his future, we expect Mr Long to request custody, but we will have to be certain that's the best solution for the lad, and that judgement will be made on certain criteria.'

'Well,' interjected Sam, 'surely the DNA tests have proved that he is the lad's biological father?'

'That is true,' Mandy replied, 'but we will still have to be convinced that he is the best person to provide a home and a future for the boy. As I understand it, he lives on a canal boat, which may not be the best place to raise a growing boy.'

'But he must be returned to his father!' Sam exclaimed forcefully. 'If he isn't, all this tragedy will have been for nothing!'

'The other issue of course, is that in finding out that Mr Long is his father, he will also need to be told that Ms Cookson wasn't his biological mother and that she had abducted him from his real parents. None of this will be easy for the lad and it has to be taken a step at a time.'

Alex, who had been listening quietly to this exchange, agreed,

'You're right Mandy, and I don't envy you your job. Anyway, I must be on my way. If there's anything you need from me, here's my card. Just ring me, anytime.'

When Alex had left, Sam offered to order a takeaway for himself and Mandy, and Archie if he was able to eat something. Mandy went upstairs and knocked quietly on Archie's door. There was no reply and after knocking again she called,

'Archie, may I come in?'

There was a muffled reply which sounded more like a grunt. She slowly opened the door.

'Hello Archie, I'm Mandy.'

The boy was lying face down on his bed and didn't even look up when she entered the room.

'I'm so sorry about your mum, Archie,' Mandy said gently.

There was no reply, but he shifted uncomfortably and punched his pillow.

'Do you want to talk?' Mandy persevered.

Still nothing.

'Can I get you something to eat? Sam's ordering a pizza, what kind do you like?'

Nothing.

'OK Archie, I can see you'd like to be alone right now, but if you would like to eat something or have a drink, just come down when you feel like it. I'll give you a shout when the pizzas arrive anyway.'

With that, Mandy quietly left.

Archie was feeling numb now. He still couldn't believe what had happened. It seemed like he was having a bad dream and that any moment he would wake up and run downstairs to find his mum cooking tea in the kitchen. He had no idea who this Mandy person was. No one had told him. And what about Sam? She hadn't even come up to see him, just leaving that to a perfect stranger. Nothing made any sense anymore, so it was safer not to think anything at all. But one thought he couldn't shut out. He wanted Trixie, but he had no idea where she was. His heart ached for her trusting face and warm body. They had told him she would be here tomorrow. Maybe things would feel better then.

Half an hour later the noise of a motorbike outside, followed by the ringing of the doorbell told him the pizza delivery man had arrived. Archie realised he hadn't eaten for hours, and in spite of himself, he was suddenly very hungry. Sam was laying the table and looked up when Archie entered the kitchen. Her face tensed and tears filled her eyes as she said,

'Archie, I'm so sorry!'

Archie didn't reply, just nodding, trying to hold back the tears.

'Come and sit down, Archie, and help yourself,' Mandy invited.

For some unknown reason this made him mad. Who was this person, asking him to sit down in his own house? Nothing to do with her, he thought. They ate their pizza and chips in silence. Just three strangers thrown together, grief, guilt and feelings of inadequacy were the spectres at the feast. They were all relieved when it was over.

Mandy suggested that Archie might like to take a bath before bed and offered to run it for him.

'I can do it myself,' he said, and stomped off up the stairs. That was the last they saw of him until the next morning.

***

Sam was tossing and turning all night. When she did snatch an hour or two it was full of dreams of Alice and images of her struggling to escape from the sinking car. At first, she blamed herself for everything that had happened in the last few days, convinced she had caused her death, and she felt that nothing and nobody would ever convince her of anything any different.

She wondered what would happen to Archie now. Surely, he would go to live with Jack. She couldn't understand how anyone could think he wouldn't. But the Social Worker hadn't seemed too sure. He just had to go back to his dad, or all this horrible mess would have been for nothing. Then the thought struck her that once Alice had recognised Jack she couldn't have gone on as before. In her mind, and probably it was also a fact, Jack wouldn't rest until he'd got his son back. No, she thought, this story had begun eleven years earlier on a beach, when Alice had seen a little boy who she'd convinced herself was her child.

In actual fact of course, it had begun two years earlier. The police had told him about the tiny baby which her parents had insisted was put up for adoption. It had been snatched from her arms by the people who should have loved and supported her. No doubt they had thought they were doing the right thing, but the road to hell and all that ..., and now it had ended for her, hundreds of miles away, in the cold waters of a Scottish loch. As she lay there, all this going through her mind, she heard the dawn chorus start up outside the window, telling her another day without Alice was beginning.

Chapter Twenty-Eight

Alex had arrived home the night before, utterly drained, at eight o'clock. Dave knew immediately the trip to Scotland had not ended well. Normally she didn't discuss work with him, but what had happened was too huge not to share it. Once the kids had finished supper and retired to their rooms as usual, Dave had said,

'So come on, it looks like you've got some unburdening to do.'

So, Alex had spent the next hour going through the tragic events of the past couple of days and how she was trying very hard not to feel responsible in some way for the boy losing his mother.

'But she wasn't, was she, his mother I mean? At least now the boy will be able to know his own dad and the truth about what happened to his birth mother. She was the one who had decided to run off with him again. That choice was hers. Your job was to stop her and return the boy to his father. The story isn't over yet, and only when it is, will you be able to judge if it was all for the best.'

'I'm sure you're right, it just doesn't feel like it right now.'

'Come here love,' he said gently before enfolding her in his arms. 'You did your job, and did it well, as you always do. Come on, time for bed. Leave these pots 'till the morning, I think you need some TLC,' he went on, smiling down at her.

'I love you, Dave Scott. You always help me to keep things in proportion.'

'Yep, that's my job, and one I'm pretty good at! Come on,' he went on, leading her by the hand up the stairs.

The next morning, Alex had decided that even though it was Sunday, she must drive over to Bristol. She had promised to let the Whiteheads know if and when she found their daughter. Well, she'd certainly found her but now someone had to tell them that she was dead, and how it happened. She could have sent Sally or Neil but felt this was the one thing she could do for Cookson now. At least her parents would know what had happened to her and they may want to go to the funeral in due course. They may also be interested to see the boy she had been raising as her own for eleven years, although of course he was no relation to them. Still, it may give them some comfort to see what a fine young man she had nurtured.

Before she left she checked in with Dorothy and Ted. Her mother answered,

'Hello love, you're back then?'

'Yes Mum, I got back last night.'

'Dad told me you were going up to Scotland. How did it go,' Dorothy asked quickly.

'Oh you know, with this job it's seldom straight-forward. In fact it was rather harrowing.'

'I'm sorry about that love, still perhaps you can relax a bit today.'

'I wish! I just have a couple of loose ends to tie up. In fact I'm just leaving for Bristol shortly but I wanted to check up how you are. Dad said you'd been a bit tired lately.

'Oh I'm alright, he fusses too much!'

'So he should! You've looked after him enough over the years, now it's your turn to be spoilt a bit! Anyway, do take care Mum and I'll try to get down in a week or two. Let me know how your next check up goes, won't you?'

'Yes of course love, and don't worry, you've got enough on your plate with the family and that job of yours.'

'OK Mum, I'd better get off now. Give my love to Dad.'

'I will, love to everybody up there.'

Alex was a little uneasy after she'd put the phone down. She felt sure Dorothy was up to her old tricks, keeping something from her. As she was driving to Bristol, she was thinking about how precious mothers are; they're always there, until, one day, they're not. Archie knew all about that. She determined she must get down to Tidmouth sometime in the next few weeks.

***.

It wasn't an easy meeting. Mrs Whitehead was utterly devastated, having believed that soon she may be able to be reunited with her daughter, even in such dreadful circumstances. Mr Whitehead didn't display much emotion, although Alex could see that he was struggling not to react. Of course, they had some questions and Alex answered them as well as she could.

'What will happen to the boy,' Mrs Whitehead asked finally.

'Well hopefully he will be returned to his father, but you know what Social Services are like, they'll still have to vet him to make sure he's a fit and proper person and in a good position to look after him.'

Mr Whitehead offered her a cup of tea, but Alex declined, saying she would have to get back. She promised to let them have details of the funeral once it was announced, then left for the office.

***

As she drove, she was mulling over the case. Obviously as Cookson was dead, there was no crime to be prosecuted, so that particular ship had now sailed. There was also no longer a suspect in the earlier abduction. Alex felt this was rather unsatisfactory from Jack Long's perspective. No one would ever pay the price for ruining his life.

She decided to call round to speak to Jack Long to put him in the picture. He would need to prepare to win custody of his son, and from what Mandy had said the previous evening that may not be straightforward.

When she arrived at the Lady Louise, Jack, as usual was sitting on the roof, painting.

'Hello Inspector,' he called down. 'Is there news?'

'There is,' she replied, 'Can I come aboard?'

When they were sitting down, Alex began, 'Well the good news is that your son is home safe and sound.'

'That's amazing news, thank you so much!'

'Well, it's not all good, I'm afraid. Ms Cookson wasn't so lucky,' she added, and then went on to explain exactly what had happened in Scotland.

All of Jack's concern was for Toby.

'Poor lad, he must be absolutely devastated and utterly confused. How much does he know, by the way, about me and what happened all those years ago?'

'Not very much at all actually, unless Cookson had already told him, but I don't think she had. He seemed to have no idea why she was running away from us.'

'OK, well I guess Social Services are already involved, so I can see that I'd better step up my game now. I've already put the boat up for sale and put my name down on one of those two-bedroom mobile homes on the site at the edge of town, so that's a start.'

'Of course, this will mean that there can be no further investigations or convictions into your son's abduction, either now or in the past. Not a very satisfactory outcome from your point of view, I imagine,' Alex pointed out.

'That's true, of course,' Jack replied. 'It is so sad for the lad to lose the only mother he's ever known, and I wouldn't have wished this on him, but in fact, it does actually simplify things as far as I'm concerned. If Cookson had still been around, he may have been unable to accept me and may have felt he was being made to choose between us. And of course, Cookson may in fact have ended up in prison, which would have been tough on Toby, and he may have blamed me for it.'

'Well, it's good that you can see it like that. I can see your main concern is for your son's wellbeing, and not for revenge. Well, I must be on my way,' Alex continued, 'I just wanted you to know how things are so that you can start making your own preparations for gaining custody of Toby. If there's anything we can do to help, just let me know.'

'I will, and thanks. By the way, have you any idea when the funeral will be? That's something else that will need careful handling.'

'It will, and we won't know about that until the PM has been carried out and the body released. I'll let you know when we hear anything.'

'Thanks, and once again, I do appreciate you keeping me in the loop,' Jack concluded as he firmly shook Alex's hand.

***

Before she returned home, Alex had one last call to make. She wanted to check on how the boy was getting on and what interim arrangements had been made for him. When she arrived at the house, she found there was some kind of meeting in progress. In the drive were three cars, one was Sam Bolton's and one presumably Mandy's, and another which she decided probably belonged to someone else connected to Social Services, and so it proved to be.

Sam opened the door and asked her to go through to the lounge. There she found Archie slumped in an armchair, still looking utterly bewildered, probably unable to comprehend how his life had changed forever. Alex said hello and told him that she'd heard that Trixie was on her way down and should be here around two o'clock, all being well. He brightened slightly at the news. Poor lamb, Alex thought, he probably feels she's his only friend right now.

The senior social worker, who introduced himself as Peter Bottomley, said he had called to have a chat with Archie, to explain to him what would be happening over the next few days. Bringing Alex up to date, he said they had found a nice local foster family to look after him until longer term arrangements could be put in place. At this, Archie spoke up for the first time.

'What do you mean, longer term arrangements? What's going to happen to me?'

'Well, Archie, we will need to decide who will look after you. You obviously can't stay here. Ms Bolton is not a blood relation and has no obligation to care for you.'

Not very tactful, Alex thought with some surprise at Peter Bottomley's lack of empathy for the lad's feelings. Then things got worse. Whether through lack of experience or knowledge of the situation, he ploughed on regardless,

'Of course, it may be possible that you could go to live with your father.'

There was total silence as everyone, apart from Bottomley, considered the enormity of what he had just said.

'I don't have a father,' Archie stated with some conviction.

'Err, I mean Mr Long, of course,' Bottomley stumbled on.

'You mean Jack?'

'Err... yes of course.'

At this point Alex could stand it no longer.

'Mr Bottomley, please can I have a private word?'

By now, Bottomley had realised that the whole conversation had taken a wrong turn somewhere and he duly followed Alex through to the kitchen, where she very quickly appraised him of the situation. He was mortified. Some cock-up in the office had indeed resulted in him not being given the full facts in this complicated case. He had thought it was just as a result of a tragic accident that Archie had lost his mother and had no knowledge about any abduction either recently or in the past. He had simply been told that his biological father was Mr Long who was living in the area and would therefore be a potential carer for the boy. He was now livid that he had been put in this embarrassing situation. Their thoughts turned to the boy.

When they returned to the room, they found him quizzing Sam Bolton trying to find out what this meant. Why had that man said Jack was his dad? It didn't make sense. Why hadn't his mum told him? Why had she run away with him anyway, taking him away from Jack, if he was his dad? Sam looked completely out of her depth, and kept looking questioningly at Mandy, to see if she had any more idea of how to handle this than she had.

Archie looked from one grown up face to the next. Who could he trust to tell him the truth? Sam? She couldn't seem to give him any answers. Mandy? She just sat silently looking down at her hands. The man called Bottomley. He obviously knew something, but he didn't feel he could trust him. No, Alex was the only person in the room who was looking him in the eye.

'Please,' he said to her, 'tell me what's going on. Why did mum run away with me and if Jack is my dad, why didn't she tell me? She knew I always wanted a dad. Please, I need to understand.'

Alex knew the task of telling the lad the truth had landed at her door, but she had no intention of washing this particular bit of dirty washing in public, and gently said,

'Of course Archie, but not here. Let's go up to your room so that we can talk.'

Chapter Twenty-Nine

'Archie,' Alex began, 'what I'm going to tell you will be difficult for you to hear, but I think you deserve, and indeed, you need to know, the truth. I think it would have been better if we could have left this for a little while until you were perhaps more able to deal with it. But that's not going to be possible now, is it?'

'No, I need to know now. I couldn't understand why mum took us away. It didn't make any sense. Now it seems like there are things I need to know that will explain it all, so please, tell me everything.'

'Well, the story begins a long time ago Archie, around the time you were born, in fact. Your mum, Alice was sixteen when she had a little baby, but because she was so young, she couldn't keep him and he was given up for adoption. Alice was very sad about that and one day saw you with your dad, Jack, on the beach. She became convinced that you were the baby that they had taken away from her and made the decision to take you back.'

'You mean she stole me from Jack!' Archie exclaimed.

'Well, I'm sure Alice didn't think of it like that. She was convinced that you were hers.'

'Didn't I have a real mum?' Archie said suddenly.

'You did, Archie, she was called Grace Long.'

'Where is she now?'

'Very sadly, she died many years ago Archie.'

'Did Jack try to find me?'

'Of course, they searched high and low for you, but could never find out where you'd gone or who had taken you. Jack did however, suspect that it may have been Alice because he'd seen her watching you on the beach. He had left your pushchair outside the corner shop while he popped inside, and Alice saw you there and simply walked away with you before Jack came out.'

Archie now sat in silence, trying to make sense of it all. So, his mum was never his mum. She was the person who had stolen him from Jack! Some things now began to slot into place. Now he understood that when Alice had seen Jack when they picked him up from the boatyard, she must have recognised him. She must also have realised that he had recognised her too, and she probably guessed that he would go to the police to tell them. Then he thought about how his re-lationship with Jack had become so important to him. He had always felt drawn to him and now he knew why. He also knew why she had run away. He wasn't sure, but kidnapping him like that must be against the law and if she'd been caught, she may have been sent to prison.

Anger now began to bubble up inside him. How could she trick him like that? Telling him he had no dad, when all the time, his dad had been looking for him! She can't have really loved him after all.

'How could she have done that, taken me away from my own mum and dad?' he asked of no one in particular.

'You must try not to think too badly of her Archie. She was obviously not well and had convinced herself she was your mum. She loved you and cared for you all these years, didn't she? As for running away, yes that was wrong of her, but she probably couldn't face losing you, which she understood would happen if she was found out.'

'Does Jack know I'm his?'

'Yes, he does now. I think he had suspected it when he saw the birthmark on your back, but of course after you went missing, we did carry out DNA tests which confirmed it.'

'And does he want me? He did say I couldn't live with him on the boat.'

'Well, he told me he's selling the boat to buy a mobile home so that if you wanted to be with him and the Social Services agreed, there would be room for you there.'

'And Trixie too?' Archie asked without any hesitation, then struck by another thought, 'Was I always Archie?'

'No, you used to be Toby Long.' Alex told him.

'Right, Toby Long. That feels weird.'

'I'm sure it does. Look love, this is an awful lot for you to take in. You need to take some time to process it all. You've still got to get over what happened to your mum yet.'

'But she wasn't my mum, was she?'

'No, but your relationship with her is an important part of your life and always will be. She made you the person you are today and whatever else she did or didn't do, in the end you must respect her for that.'

'Can I see Jack now please?' he asked in a tone that told Alex he wouldn't take no for an answer.

'Let's go downstairs now and perhaps I'll be able to take you over to him, although I'm sure it won't be possible for you to move in with him straight away. There will be formalities to sort out first.'

Bottomley wasn't keen on allowing Alex to take him to see Jack. She explained that he was now fully aware that Jack was his father but understood that nothing could be finalised yet. He needed to see him. In fact, Alex pointed out, he had a right to see him. Finally, Bottomley agreed as long as Mandy accompanied them.

As Alex was driving them over to the canal, she was thinking that perhaps Bottomley's error had been for the best. The lad had taken the news with a maturity she hadn't realised she possessed. She supposed the relationship he already had with Jack had been a huge factor in that. They parked up in the canal carpark and started to walk along the towpath. Archie broke into a run as he saw Ben tied up beside the Lady

Louise. Hearing the fuss Ben was making, Jack's head and shoulders emerged from inside the cabin, and he saw Toby running towards him.

Without hesitation, Toby ran along the gangplank and jumped down into the cockpit, throwing himself at Jack, who realised immediately that the lad knew. Without either of them uttering a word they clung together for several moments. The boy was where he belonged, and the father had his son back. If Alex had ever doubted she'd done the right thing in finding him and bringing him home, at that moment, all her misgivings disappeared and she knew exactly why she did this job.

***

After giving them several minutes together, Alex had to remind Toby that he wouldn't be able to stay with Jack yet, but it was hard to part the two of them just as they had found each other. Jack insisted on returning with them, so that he could speak with Mr Bottomley to work out what was to happen next.

When they arrived back at the house Mr Bottomley explained to them both that foster parents had been arranged for Toby and that they lived only a few streets away. Jack would be able to visit him regularly until a more permanent solution could be found. He invited Jack to attend a meeting the following day at the Social Services offices to discuss things in more detail.

Toby wasn't happy with this arrangement, but Jack gently explained to him that it would be for the best right now, and that he would be doing all he could to speed things up, and he was sure they would be together eventually.

Feeling that her job was done, and that Toby was now in good hands, Alex explained that she had to leave. As she was going Jack strode over and shook her hand vigorously, saying that he was so grateful that she had brought Toby back safely.

***

As she drove home Alex pondered on the drama of the last few days. So much had happened. It seemed unbelievable that only yesterday she had been in Scotland, involved in the car chase that had resulted in Alice Cookson's death. Could she have done any-thing differently, she wondered, something that may have avoided that tragic outcome? That poor boy, losing his mother and gaining a father all in the space of a few hours. She had been amazed how well he had coped with it all.

Now Alex's thoughts turned to her own mother and as they did so, there was the familiar flutter of anxiety in the pit of her stomach. When she'd last spoken to her dad, she'd definitely detected the worry in his voice, even though he'd done his best to hide it. Could it be that the cancer was back? It was too late to contact them now, but she determined to ring the next morning and to plan to get down to Tidmouth to see for herself exactly how things were with them.

As she pulled up outside the house, the light in the lounge told her that Dave was still up and with some relief she turned her key in the lock, and entered her personal sanctuary, away from the troubles of the world.

'Hello love,' Dave greeted her as she entered the lounge, 'you look done in.'

'Well, it's been quite a day. I couldn't cope with too many like that, I can tell you.'

'Feet up and a glass of wine then?'

'Absolutely! You always know exactly what a girl needs at a time like this!'

'Wine isn't the only thing you need,' he said, folding her in his arms and holding her close.

'I love you, Dave Scott,' she murmured.

Dave simply replied, 'I know.' That was all that was needed.

Chapter Thirty

The funeral was a strange affair given the conflicting emotions that most people were experiencing. Sam Bolton was there, of course. Still feeling guilty, she felt the least she could do was to organise a decent funeral for Alice. In fact, she had to be the one to make all the arrangements, being the nearest thing Alice had to a functioning 'next of kin'.

The Whitehads never got involved and in fact, never even went to see their daughter at the Chapel of Rest. No-one really expected them to turn up, but in the end, they sat at the back of the crematorium and only Alex and Neil realised who they were. Alex had meant to introduce the boy to them, but when she turned round after the service, intending to suggest it to them, they had already left. Alice had left a will, leaving everything to Archie of course, so no further contact was made with them. There were also a few of Alice's colleagues from school at the crematorium, but apart from Sam, no other friends, or relatives. Jack was there simply to support his son. It was a sad reflection on an insular life.

Social Services agreed that Jack should eventually take charge of the boy. Of course, there were a few hurdles to overcome. He had needed to provide a home for Toby and find himself a job so that he could support him, but the prospect of creating a future for them both gave him all the incentive he needed. Toby was temporarily placed with a foster family, who had been happy to take Trixie as well.

Although Jack was able to see them often, it was obvious that Toby needed the long-term stability of a home of his own. Understandably, the lad was still grieving for Alice Cookson, while at the same time trying to come to terms with the anger he felt at having been stolen away from his own family. It took every ounce of Jack's understanding and empathy to help him to process all this. He knew the boy could easily become bitter and unhappy if it wasn't handled well.

Of course, Jack had had to cope with his own anger at Cookson, who had actually ruined his life too, and that wasn't easy, but he knew he also had to avoid bitterness if he was to help his son. So, all in all, it had been quite an emotional journey, one which, although not yet complete, was one they were making together and that made the effort worthwhile.

He soon found a buyer for the boat and with the money bought the mobile home he'd had his eye on, thinking it would be ideal for the two of them and the dogs. So after just three months they moved in together.

***

One weekend not long afterwards, for some reason, Jack had felt the need to take Toby back to where it all began. Now the sun was sinking towards the horizon, its rays bouncing off the surface of the water to skim across the wet sand, where two dogs and a boy splashed in the wavelets as they gently ebbed and flowed. It had been a perfect day.

They had needed this, to get away from reminders of the traumas of the past few months; to find some peace and space just to be together and, he supposed, to find some kind of closure. However, Jack couldn't help letting his thoughts wander backwards a little, to the sheer joy of that moment when Toby had thrown himself into his arms and he knew, beyond any doubt, that he finally had his son back.

Of course, the joy was tempered with some sadness, at the fact that Grace would never enjoy that feeling, and regret that he had missed so much of his son's life. But the joy of finding him again outweighed all of that.

He knew there might be difficult times ahead. No boy could go through what Toby had suffered without it having some effect on him. But Jack also knew that with the love and security he would provide for him, Toby would get through it and grow into the fine young man his mother would have been proud of.

END

About the Author

About the Author

Marilyn was born in Oldham, Lancashire, England but has lived in various places across the UK. After a business career she began creating and publishing books for her husband and various private clients before embarking on her own writing career. She has published four books, three of them family mystery and suspense novels. Coalbrookdale is a historical novel.

She now lives in Bedford with her husband. She has just embarked a fifth book, a sequel to Coalbrookdale, titled 'The Wrekin' which will be published in 2023.

For more information, please visit her website at www.spellbrooktales.com.

Other Books by the Author

Karma, A Mystery in Paris

Karma is a story of mystery and suspense set largely in 1970's Paris. A fatal accident and chance discovery propel Adrienne on her journey as she searches for the reason why her mother, Janey, disappeared from the family home ten years previously. The story she reveals spans three decades and has its roots in the Nazi occupation of the city during the 1940's and the evils perpetrated.The consequences of those events echo down the years and little by little we begin to understand why Janey never came home. It is a story with many twists and turns, the shocking conclusion delivering a certain natural justice.

Secrets and Lives

When Joan gave up her baby for adoption in 1972, she could have had no idea what consequences would follow, decades later. When her son, now a man, re-enters her life without warning, tragedy ensues. The life John was forced to lead has left its mark on him, and even the love of his sister Sophie, living a comfortable life in Bath, cannot undo the harm already done.

This is a domestic thriller exploring nature v nurture, sibling rivalry and abandonment issues. It is a page turner, guaranteed to surprise right to the very end.

Coalbrookdale: The Bangham Family Story

This is a work of fiction based on the life of Joseph Bangham, who lived in the Severn Gorge three hundred years ago. He worked for the Coalbrookdale ironworks when Abraham Darby was perfecting the use of coal in the production of iron and as the technology spread, industry thrived.

The lives of Joseph and his family change fundamentally as the agricultural evolves into the industrial way of life. The book traces the story of the Bangham family as they move from Banghams Wood where they have been coppicing for decades across the Gorge to Coalbrookdale and a life regulated not by the seasons but by the demands of the furnaces. As with any family story there is joy as well as tragedy, all played out against the backdrop of the often brutal 18th Century in England, when a child could be transported to America or even hanged for poaching a rabbit.

All Marilyn's books are available from Amazon and

most other online bookstores. For more information, visit www.spellbrooktales.com

CPSIA information can be obtained
at www.ICGtesting.com
Printed in the USA
BVHW041141301122
653109BV00004B/107